Are you Lost?

by

Fay Wentworth

First published 2017

Text copyright © 2017 Fay Wentworth

ISBN - 13: 978-1539886716

ISBN - 10: 1539886719

Acknowledgements

I would like to thank my husband, *Bobby*, for his unfailing patience and support

My thanks to:
Minster Scribblers and fellow members of the *RNA* for their constructive comments on my initial drafts
Don Millar for his constructive editing and advice
Judy Pugh for her inspiration when a name eluded me
Mike Waygood for sharing his knowledge of building regulations

I cannot leave out my family, who stoically bear the burden of a mother who is a writer and therefore, sometimes, 'away with the fairies'

Cover by *Don Millar*

Part One – *Every time you die…*

'Today,' Ethan Randle thought, as he sliced chunks of meat into the bowl, 'today she will come.'

He thought of his soul-mate, devouring the blood-dripping lumps, and he smiled. A feast to enjoy, and he would.

'Lily', the name wafted and clung in his memory. 'Lily,' he whispered and a surge of triumph seared his mind. At last the interminable wait was over.

* * * * * * * * * *

She had passed the house before recognition hit her. Slamming on the brakes, Freya slid onto the grass verge. Her heart was hammering. She took a deep breath. Backing up, she drove the car into the narrow layby opposite and turned off the engine, her hands shaking. Clutching the steering wheel, she twisted in her seat, staring at the stone building. A paint-peeled wooden sign hung crookedly, *Leofric Farm*.

Built in stone, the side wall nearest the road was windowless, and the ragged lawn that fronted the house was without adornment. No pots of early pansies, no trays of polyanthus, nothing to acknowledge the beginning of spring. An ancient apple tree reared above the roof, its branches swaying in the breeze, the leaves brushing the dark tiles.

Freya stepped out of the car, closing the door quietly. She stood, stretching; it had been a long journey and it wasn't over yet. She really didn't have time to linger. Her eyes swept the house and the dry stone wall separating it from the road, lichen covered and tumble-down, where stones were displaced.

Her eyes were drawn to a large bone in the middle of the yard, chewed and yellowed. She looked around nervously.

"Can I help you?" The man's voice cut through her uneasiness and she jumped. He was standing in the yard, the door open behind him.

"Are you lost?"

She nodded. Yes, she was lost; there was no doubt about that. But not in the sense he meant.

Tall, his body taut, his hair, the colour of ripe corn, fell in waves to his shoulders. He reminded her of someone she once knew. She searched her memory, but a name eluded her. She scanned his face, and his eyes, reflecting gold from the sun, held hers. For a moment she felt a tingle of shock and... recognition? Her heart pounding, she felt a yearning deep in her soul.

'I know this man'. The words drifted through her mind like shadows in a breeze. She cleared her throat.

"Do you live here?" She ventured across the road as he nodded.

"Were you expecting to find someone else?" His smile was humorous. "Ethan Randle," he bowed slightly, "at your service."

She shook her head, trying to regain her composure. "No, of course not. I'm a stranger in these parts." She held out her hand. "Freya...

6

Freya Elisandre. It's just… the house looks familiar."

"Freya – of course, Freya." He stared at her for a moment. "Perhaps you'd like to look around?" He was grinning now and she blushed, shaking her head.

"Pity." His voice was teasing. "Another time maybe?"

Once again, he captured her gaze. Disconcerted, she bit her lip.

"Now," his voice became brisk, "can I help you find whoever you're looking for? As you can see," he gestured beyond her, "the road ends here."

"I'm heading for Hereford. The signpost indicated up here?"

"It's confusing. There are two left turns and the signpost on the other side is slightly off-course."

"Very annoying."

"For those in a hurry! At least there's room to turn round here. There was a *Dead End* sign at the end of my road. A lorry cut the corner – no more sign. The council have promised to replace it…" He shrugged.

Thanking him, she climbed back into the car, catching her skirt in the door as she hurriedly closed it and fastened her seat belt. With a wave and a slight smile, she executed a clumsy turn and sped off down the road and round the next corner where she stopped in a gateway, shaking.

Taking a deep breath, she laid her head on her arms on the steering wheel and calmed her thoughts. She couldn't possibly recognise the house, or its occupant. She'd never been to

Herefordshire before. She searched her memory. There had to be somewhere similar in her past. All the same, she had an urge to see inside, to see if the rooms were as she imagined in her head…

She leaned back in her seat and smiled wryly. She was having a 'Clara moment'. She would tell her mother when she phoned later, perhaps she would have an answer. Freya sighed and shook her head. Starting the car, she set off down the country lane.

Outside the house, Ethan Randle stared after the retreating car, watching the dust settle on the narrow road. Excitement stirred adrenalin and he smiled. She didn't know it yet, but she had come home.

A frown creased his brow and his eyes became sombre, hardening as his mind reached into the past. An interminable time ago. Nothing must stand in his way this time; and no one would defeat him now.

Freya breathed a sigh of relief as she reached the main road. She took the next left and she was back on route. She was tired. It had been an early start from Cornwall and the motorway had been busier than she expected.

Thankfully pulling into the hotel car park, she humped her case from the boot and wheeled it to Reception. They were expecting her.

The transfer to the Bull Hotel in Hereford had seemed a dream opportunity. Thankful to escape Bodmin, she had accepted the job with alacrity. And here she was, exhausted and confused, unpacking in her small room on the top floor.

The next morning, Freya felt more cheerful. The sun streamed through her window and, as she leaned on the sill, she could see people scurrying to work on the pavement below. The hotel sign swung heavily from the wall. A Hereford Bull watched with melting eyes as the world came alive. The building was ancient, built in the black and white style of the area, great oak beams holding the structure together.

Dressing hurriedly, she sped downstairs to the breakfast room and stood looking around, wondering who to approach. A tall man headed in her direction.

"Freya Elisandre? I'm Mark Brinton, assistant manager." He smiled and Freya responded. A good looking man, about her age, he had an air of confidence and an elegance that she admired.

"Come and grab some breakfast, then I'll show you around. We've been managing the Reception desk between us and it's been rather difficult, so we're delighted to see you." He guided her to a table and motioned to the self-service display. "Help yourself; we eat before the guests emerge."

Freya poured coffee and reached for toast, glancing around as she settled at the table. The atmosphere was comfortable and cosy and Freya felt immediately at home.

The Reception desk was mahogany, highly polished, and Freya soon mastered the filing and booking system under Mark's patient guidance. By lunch time she felt confident enough to answer the telephone.

"My office is down the corridor," Mark said. "Any queries, don't hesitate to ask."

"Thanks." Freya stood alone and nervously waited for her first visitor.

Within a week, Freya was enjoying herself. Mark was attentive and helpful and she wondered about his personal circumstances. She studied him from a distance. He was attractive, there was no doubt about that but, somehow, her heart remained steady in his presence.

She sighed. She'd had boyfriends in the past, several; after all, she was twenty six, but never had she felt that attraction that allowed her to settle into a relationship. She had a yearning inside, for what she knew not, but a yearning that longed to be satisfied – if she could just meet the right man.

Saturday was her day off and she decided to explore. Heading out from Hereford she followed meandering country lanes, stopped at a village café for lunch and then, coming to the familiar left turn, she hesitated. She had to see Leofric Farm again, see Ethan Randle and find out if her imagination was right about the interior of the old farm.

"So…" he leaned on the gate, "are you lost again?" His smile was teasing and his eyes twinkled. Freya blushed as she stepped out of the car.

"I'm exploring, finding my way around."

"Please," he opened the gate, "come in for a moment."

Freya hesitated, fighting the urge to run away. A frisson of tension crept down her spine and she felt her heart flip as his eyes held hers. Surely she had seen this man before?

She locked the car and followed him across the grass, stopping as she faced the door. Taking a deep breath, she turned and looked at him.

"I think I've been here before, perhaps when I was young... I remember the house inside – I think."

"Describe it." He stood between her and the door, his gaze quizzical.

"Beyond the door, a hallway." She closed her eyes for a moment. "On the left, a sitting room, maybe used as a study; on the right a comfortable living room. The kitchen is at the back, everyone congregates there, it's warm and cosy... How am I doing?" Her voice trembled.

"Spot on!" He laughed and held open the door. Freya caught her breath as she stepped inside. She *had* been here before. She glanced in the rooms to the left and right as she followed Ethan down the hall into the large kitchen. At one end a wooden table and chairs, a dresser full of miss-matched plates and, at the other end, an Aga, two easy chairs placed on the side. There were no pictures, but a photograph on the dresser caught her eye. A young lady in an old-fashioned dress stared at the camera, her eyes wide and startled. Ethan followed her gaze, but made no comment as he reached for the kettle.

"Coffee?" Freya nodded as her gaze swept the room. Suddenly shaky, she sat. "I was right," she whispered.

He nodded, "And upstairs – the bedrooms?" His eyes were teasing and she laughed uncomfortably. "Three and a bathroom," she replied quickly. "Fairly standard."

"You were here when you were a child?" They were sitting either side the Aga, the warmth gentle.

"I don't know," Freya replied. "I know my great-grandfather lived around here…"

"George Winton," he said quietly.

"How did you know that?"

He shrugged. "When you live in an area like this, stories of bygone families are a major talking point."

"Papa George, my great-grandfather," she said. "And his sister, Clara. He had a daughter, Molly, but she married a Cornish man, Albert. I didn't think we'd ever been back."

"Your mother?"

"She may have been – I'll ask her. Perhaps she brought me here… How long have you lived here?"

"All my life."

"Oh, then you'd know if my mother had visited."

"Maybe, I don't remember. We get the occasional lost soul."

She smiled. "And I'm one."

"You're different. We've been waiting for you."

She looked at him sharply, discomforted by his words, but he was smiling and she shuddered, aware of her sensitivity. There was something about this place – she must ask her mother.

She stood up, suddenly anxious to leave. "I must go." She held out her hand.

"So soon?" He held her hand in his and she felt an electricity spark between them.

Pulling her fingers from his grasp, she turned

and almost ran down the hall. Opening the door, she took a deep breath of fresh air and blinked in the sunshine. From across the yard came the rumble of a growl.

"Please come back again." He shut the gate behind her and she was aware of his gaze as she started the car and sped off down the lane. He was still watching as she rounded the corner. Her mind was in turmoil. There had to be a simple explanation. Pulling into a layby, she reached for her mobile and dialled her mother's number.

"Hi, Mum."

"Freya. How are you, how's Herefordshire?" Elspeth asked.

"Umm, different; pretty. The hotel's great. I think I'll enjoy it there."

"That's good."

"Mum, did we ever come to Herefordshire?"

"Yes, we did once, when you were small. We took a holiday and explored the countryside."

So, she had been before. Freya thought for a moment. "Did you find the house that Papa George lived in?" There was a sudden crackling on the line and Freya looked at her phone in exasperation. The signal in Herefordshire wasn't good; due to the surrounding Welsh hills, Mark had said. "Mum, Mum, are you there, can you hear me?" More spluttering and Freya sighed. She'd ring again later.

Freya closed her phone and sat staring at the swaying hedges. It was pretty countryside, there was no doubt; green and lush, the Welsh Mountains and Hay Bluff towering on the horizon. Yes, she liked it here. She was making too much of her sensitive feelings. Her 'Clara moments' were taking control. She smiled wryly. Back to work - she was on duty that evening and perhaps that would bring her imagination into line. She had been here before, even if she was too young to remember and it was surprising what memories lodged in a child's mind.

Reassured, she started the car and headed back to Hereford.

Ethan Randle sat lost in thought, his fingers gently caressing the photograph of the young lady that he had reached down from the dresser. A wistful smile touched his face and he gazed at the image.

"It's time for you to come home, my love," he whispered and, with a sigh, he leaned back in the chair, the picture resting on his knees.

Freya concentrated on her work. She was enjoying it and Mark was cheerful company, often joining her for meals.

"I really must take some time to have a look around Hereford," Freya said as she sipped her water. "There's so much history to the place. I bought a book from the shop by the Cathedral – it's fascinating reading. And I'd love to find the farm my family owned."

"Your great-grandfather?"

She nodded. "My great, great-grandfather, Harold Winton, bought it in the 1800s, but it's Papa George I'm really interested in and his sister, Clara. Apparently Clara was psychic!" She giggled.

"Useful," he replied with a straight face.

"Mum says I'm like her; but I think I've just

got a strong imagination!"

"Well, there's certainly enough history in these parts to feed your mind."

She smiled, thinking of Leofric Farm. Psychic or sensitive? She didn't know.

"I'll willingly show you around Hereford." Mark leaned over the table grinning at her. "I'll have a look at the rota; see if I can wangle some time off together."

"That would be great, Mark, I'll look forward to it."

It was to be several days before Mark could fulfil his promise and show Freya around Hereford. But, that Saturday, both had a day off and, after breakfast, they set off through High Town. It was Market day and the square was filled with stalls loaded with local produce, crafts and tempting wares. The smell of strong coffee mingled with the aroma of cooking doughnuts and Freya sniffed appreciatively, Mark laughed and guided her to an alley that led into the cobbled Church Street, where timbered shops overhung the walkway and doorbells rang. The passed through ancient iron railings into the grassy grounds of the majestic cathedral.

"I'll take you in there," Mark said as they wandered passed the great oak doors. "I want to show you the chained library and, of course, the famous Mappa Mundi. But not today, it's a shame to waste the sunshine."

They carried on to the river and then Mark slowed his pace as they followed the path that meandered under weeping willows and oaks. The sun glinted on the water and ducks and moorhens vied for scraps thrown by children. Elegant swans looked on disdainfully, gliding through the reeds and floating silently with the current.

Mark and Freya walked in silence for a while, Freya marvelling at the tranquillity.

"It's beautiful, Mark," she said. "So peaceful."

It seemed natural for Mark to take her hand and, as they rounded a bend and left the playing families behind, he pulled her down beside him on a wooden bench.

"So, what do you think of Herefordshire so far?"

Freya smiled. "I like it. I can understand why Papa George loved it. It's a shame the family had to move away."

"Was there no one to take over the farm?"

Freya shook her head. "Grandma Molly went on holiday to Cornwall and met Grandad. Great Nana Bea passed away and, when Papa George died, Leofric was sold to a neighbour who wanted the land. I didn't know the house had been sold separately."

"What happened to Clara?"

Freya frowned. "That seems to be a bit of a family mystery. Apparently she disappeared soon after Papa George was invalided out of the army. There was a man around at the time, but what happened to him, I don't know."

"A mystery lover. How exciting!"

Freya laughed. "Perhaps I'll find out one day. I've never really thought about it, but maybe Grandma would know."

"Where was the farm?"

Freya shrugged. "I thought maybe it was Leofric Farm." She hesitated. "It looked familiar when I stopped there."

"That old ruin?"

"Hardly a ruin," Freya replied. "Run down, yes, but not ruined, yet. Rather beautiful really."

He raised his eyebrows. "Beautiful? Well, I suppose it was, once."

Freya looked surprised. "It's fascinating."

"If you like old ruins! Give me a new detached with mod cons any day."

"Oh, you're just a spoil sport!" Freya laughed. "I think the house is wonderful; atmospheric and truly beautiful." She sighed.

Mark looked puzzled. "Well, I've only seen it once, I took a wrong turning…"

"Me too!" Freya laughed.

"But apparently it's haunted."

"Haunted?"

"So the locals say. The kids go there at night to scare themselves, but I don't think anyone's come to harm yet."

Freya was silent, wondering what Ethan would think of local lads creeping around his house at night. No, the house hadn't seemed haunted.

Admittedly, the feeling of familiarity was creepy, as was the longing that filled her, the wanting to return, to see Ethan again…

She shook her head, expelling Ethan from her thoughts, and turned to Mark with a smile.

"Anyway, enough about me, tell me about the North."

"Dear old Yorkshire." He affected a strong accent and she laughed. "I love it really. It's wild and harsh, but the people are genuine. Herefordshire is gentle compared to my home. But I love it here - for a change."

17

"But you'll go home?"

"Of course. I'd like to travel around a bit first, work in other hotels. But yes, I shall go home eventually."

They sat in companionable silence for a while and then Mark pulled Freya to her feet. "We'll cut across the meadow and get some lunch in town?"

"That sounds great."

She stood looking at him for a moment and then, very slowly he lowered his face and his lips found hers in a soft kiss. He slid his arms around her back and pulled her close. She found herself responding and their kiss deepened. It was delicious; oh, so warm and comforting. As she pulled away, she felt a surge of excitement.

She touched her lips with her fingers and smiled. Mark was a lovely man, maybe…

As they turned and walked hand in hand across the grass her thoughts were confused and it was Ethan's face that filled her mind, making her heart skip a beat, and she clasped Mark's hand tightly, angry with herself.

She accepted Mark's invitations to a meal out, the cinema; he was wonderful company, they got on so well together, but… Eventually she found herself with a free afternoon. She knew Mark was working and, arguing angrily with herself, she sat in her car and started the engine.

It had been a while; perhaps she had imagined her reactions. She wanted to confirm this, she told herself as she set off for the farm; that was all, and she wanted to know if her reactions had changed since she had been in Mark's company.

She stood and looked at Leofric Farm. There was

no sign of Ethan. She was hoping to go home soon and decided to take a couple of photos to show the family. Grandma would know whether it was the right place. Fishing in her handbag for her phone she tapped the camera and watched as the farm filled the small screen. Quickly, she took some shots, moving along the road to capture different angles.

The front door swung open. Guiltily, she closed her phone and thrust it back in her bag. For some reason, she didn't want Ethan to see her taking photos. Why? She shook her head. She had no rational explanation.

Taking a deep breath, she fixed a smile on her face and swung open the gate.

"It's strange," Freya clasped her mug of tea, "how comfortable I feel in this room."

"You must have enjoyed yourself here as a child."

"I must have." She stared at him. "But why," she frowned in concentration, "why can't I remember?"

The smile hid the sorrow in his eyes. "One day you will."

She sighed. "That's what Mark said."

"Mark?" He was instantly alert, his voice sharp.

"Mark, the assistant manager," Freya explained. "He's an incomer too, from Yorkshire, helping out for the summer."

"You've told him about Leofric Farm?" Ethan was watching her, alarmed.

"Of course." Freya was startled. "Shouldn't I have?"

He shrugged and relaxed back. "Has he been here?"

Freya shook her head. "He's not interested in old ruins." She laughed. "I told him it wasn't an old ruin yet!"

Ethan stood and strode to the window. Freya studied his back, scared by the tension that had suddenly sprung between them.

He turned and his eyes narrowed as they gazed down at her. "He's friendly, this Mark?"

"Oh yes, very. He's been a tremendous help to me. We've explored Hereford - he knows the town better than I…" Her voice tailed off as his icy gaze stopped her words.

"I mean…" She stared into the cooling liquid. "He's been on hand at work – it's so busy, he's shown me around…" She was fumbling for words, for explanations of she knew not what. All she knew was that Ethan was angry and she felt afraid. Her heart hammered and her palms were damp. She slurped her drink and tea dribbled onto her wrist. Angrily, she wiped it away.

"I know Hereford better than Mark," Ethan answered softly. "After all, I'm a local!"

"Well then, you had better come and take me on another guided tour. Show me all the hidden places in your kingdom!"

A shadow passed over his face. "Maybe one day."

"Why not Friday? It's my day off." Freya snapped. Why wouldn't he leave Leofric Farm? "I want to see inside the cathedral."

Ethan stared at her for a moment, his eyes holding hers, and then shook his head.

"Then I'll have to ask Mark to take me…" She

stopped as a look of pure fury passed across Ethan's face and she shrank back from his hostility. "I was…only joking." Her voice trembled and the moment passed, fury dispelling to a wry smile. But his eyes remained cold and Freya shivered.

"I will take you, Freya, I will." His voice was soft. "But not yet. Wait for me."

She wondered why he was always busy. There seemed to be very little land to tend, a small orchard at the back, a meadow, and there were no animals. It didn't make sense. He had no vehicle; he didn't appear to work…

She shook her head. Nothing made sense. Not her obsession with Leofric Farm, her frightening attraction to Ethan, her repeated visits that left her disturbed and confused. Her inability to break the gossamer thread that drew her here and strengthened with each visit.

She felt threatened, helpless and, sometimes, very, very scared, despite the glorious feeling of exhilaration that Leofric Farm and its owner aroused in her.

"Do you ever go out, Ethan?"

"Of course!" He laughed. "I'm just too busy at the moment."

"Doing what?"

He shrugged. "The house needs some repairs, the tiles need fixing before winter…"

"But, surely, you must go to Hereford sometimes. What do you live on?"

"Anything I need is here."

"Food?"

"Deliveries."

She stared at him. He had an answer for

everything. "Aren't you lonely, by yourself?"

"Oh. I'm not alone."

"The dog." She nodded.

"Dog?" He looked startled.

"The bone in the yard? I presumed you had a dog."

Ethan rubbed his cheek. "Ah, my soul-mate," he answered quietly.

"Soul-mate?"

"His name's Daniel."

"I've never seen him, is he always shut up?"

"I'll introduce you one day, when the time is right. He's... not very friendly towards strangers."

Freya stared at him. His answers sounded logical and yet...

"I don't understand, Ethan, everything about Leofric is so... strange."

He didn't answer, a frown on his brow, his eyes concerned.

"I'd best be getting back." She stood up.

"I'm sorry." Ethan was beside her immediately, his hand restraining her arm. "Really sorry."

"Why all the mystery, Ethan? Why the anger when I talked about Mark?"

He grimaced and the twinkle returned to his eyes. "Jealous?" He gave a low chuckle.

"Jealous!" she replied. "Of what? The friendship of a colleague? Besides, you and I..." She hesitated. "Are we not just friends too?"

The electricity charged from his eyes to hers, the tawny lights glittering, capturing her, silencing her and she knew beyond doubt that a barrier had been broken. Catching her breath, she pulled her arm free and backed towards the door.

"I'm going, Ethan," she whispered. "Now."

He didn't detain her, but his eyes held hers until she felt the physical force of release as she turned away and reached for the door handle. She crossed the grass, the sound of the apple tree branches scraping the tiles echoing in her ears as she opened her car door.

"You'll come back?" Ethan had reached the gate and his mouthed words thudded on the glass.

She pushed hard on the accelerator and mud and grass spurted beneath her wheels. As she turned the corner, she glanced in the mirror. Ethan was silhouetted against the sky, his hand held out, beseeching. She clutched the steering wheel and realised she was shaking, panic-stricken, and slowly she eased her foot from the pedal and drove to the main road, her thoughts jumbled, her nerves jangling as she joined the cacophony of roaring traffic.

'You will come back.' Ethan watched until the last speck of dust fell to the roadside and then his arm slipped to his side.

He felt calmer now. He had reacted badly. But he was so afraid. Who was this Mark, helping his Freya? He had waited too long. No one, but no one, was going to come between him and Freya again. Not today or ever.

He had plans to make, solutions to find, a prize to win – and he would. Ethan Randle was not to be thwarted. Nothing was allowed to stand in his way. He needed to think – and quickly.

At last Freya managed to escape home for a long

weekend. Her mother was delighted to see her.

"Freya, how lovely. Come on in. I want to hear all about your new job and Herefordshire. How was it? Is it as beautiful as I remember? Have you found Papa George's farm?"

Freya laughed. "Wait till I get my coat off!" She followed her mother into the kitchen and relaxed onto a stool.

"Sorry – kettle's on. I'm so excited to see you."

Freya felt the comfort of familiarity wash over her. It was good to be home. She almost wished she wasn't going back…

"I've asked Grandma for lunch tomorrow," Elspeth continued. "She was going to look in a box of stuff she's got in the attic, see what she could find."

The rest of the day passed pleasantly, news exchanged, home gossip caught up on and then Freya pleaded tiredness, settling for an early night. It had been a long drive and her emotions were mixed as she laid her head on the down pillow in her old bed. She thought of Ethan, so far away now; and Mark. Somehow, it seemed as if she had been in another world and, for the moment, she had escaped. She wondered why the word 'escaped' seemed relevant and she was pondering on that as she slipped into a dreamless sleep.

Grandma Molly greeted Freya with an enveloping hug. "My, Freya, it's nice to have you home."

"Hello, lass." Grandad Albert's voice rasped as he patted her on the shoulder. "Good to see you."

After lunch they settled in the front room.

"Well, Mum," Elspeth handed out cups of tea, "did you discover any photos of your home?"

Molly shook her head. "Not of the farm. I know I had some somewhere, but heaven only knows what's happened to them. I left when I was sixteen, but I went home several times until Dad died, but... Anyway, I can tell you how to get there. The farm was up a dead-end..."

"Leofric Farm?" Freya interrupted.

"That's it!" Molly exclaimed. "You've found it?"

"I have." Freya grinned in triumph. "I knew I'd been there before, it was so familiar. I've taken photos." She reached for her phone and tapped the camera. She stared at it for a moment as she scrolled through the photos. "That's strange..." She frowned. "There's nothing here." Quickly she scanned the pictures. Photos of The Bull Hotel, the river, Hereford, even Mark slipped before her eyes, but after that – no Leofric Farm, just shots of a stone wall.

"I took them in a hurry," she said. "But I was sure..."

"There was a high stone wall between the house and the road," Molly said. "Perhaps it got in the way!" She laughed.

"High wall?" Freya stared at her. "It's falling down now. Just a heap of stones in places."

"Oh well, I expect it's been neglected."

"There was an apple tree, against the wall of the house."

"Yes, that was planted when I was a child. If it's still there it must be enormous!"

"It is." Freya smiled. "It keeps tapping on the roof."

Molly sighed. "I often wondered what happened to the old place. I don't like going back, never have, but I've thought about it. At one time I thought I would stay and run the farm but then, of course, I went on holiday and met your Grandad," she smiled across at Albert, "and I wasn't interested in anybody else's life. Very selfish of me!" She chuckled, but Freya saw the sadness in her eyes.

"Never mind," Freya said cheerfully. "Now I've found your home, I'll take some more pictures for you and you can compare it to your memories."

"I'm sure," Elspeth looked thoughtful, "I'm really sure I've never taken you there, Freya."

"You must have done, Mum. I recognised the house straight away and I could tell Ethan where the rooms were before I went in."

"Ethan?" Elspeth raised her eyebrows.

"He lives there now." Freya coloured. "I found the house by mistake, took the wrong turning, and he invited me in."

"Strange." Elspeth shook her head.

"A Clara moment!" Molly declared dramatically, and they all laughed.

"Talking of Clara…" Molly reached into her bag. "I did find a photo of her, and her journal." She held them up with a flourish.

Freya took the photo and stared at it. Surely… No! Her heart was beating rapidly and she shivered. The more she looked at Clara, smiling in the photo, her eyes twinkling, the more she was sure it was the same person that was in the photograph on Ethan's dresser; or was it? Was there a slight difference?

Her mother was looking over her shoulder. "You bear a remarkable likeness to Clara." She studied her daughter.

"Do I?" Freya studied the photo. "Perhaps a little, the features…"

"And the eyes," Elspeth said firmly. "Definitely. You've got her eyes."

Freya laid the photo on her lap and reached for the journal. It was faded leather, tied with a wilting pink ribbon.

"Have you read it, Grandma?"

"No, I could never bring myself to open it somehow and then, over time, I forgot about it."

"Can I borrow it; take it back with me to read?"

"Of course you can, dear. Take the photo as well if you want."

Freya tucked them both carefully in her bag. She had a feeling she had just discovered something important, but now was not the time to open the doors to the past.

"What happened to Clara?"

Her grandmother sighed. "Father arranged for her to go and live with a cousin up north. There was some problem with a man I gather, she needed to get away. George kept in touch."

"Did you contact her again?"

"I wrote to her, asked her to my wedding, and I kept promising to visit… And then I heard she had died. I regret that I didn't see her just once. She wouldn't come home and I know she longed to see me, never having children herself, but I was very selfish then…"

"I'm sure she understood, Grandma, and you did keep in touch. Was she happy?"

27

"I don't know, her letters were cheerful. She had a flat, a job, but she never married. I like to think she was happy."

"I wonder…" Freya sat, lost in thought.

"It was a long time ago and I was young." Her grandmother sighed. "There was too much else going on in my life."

There was silence for a while and then Elspeth jumped up, clapping her hands. "Enough of this, the past is long gone and we can't undo what is done. How about a nice cup of tea?"

Freya laughed. "Lovely, Mum, and so sensible!"

It was a pleasant weekend and Freya left reluctantly. Kissing her mother, she turned the car and sped onto the road, tears hazing her sight. Quickly wiping them away, she concentrated on her journey and wearily dragged her case into The Bull Hotel. She hadn't taken the wrong turning this time and she wasn't sure she ever wanted to see Leofric Farm again.

"How was your visit?" She and Mark were drinking coffee in their morning break.

"It was lovely to be home." Freya smiled. "I didn't realise how much I missed everybody."

Mark nodded. "I know what you mean."

"It does seem though," Freya leaned over the table, "that Leofric Farm is where Papa George and Clara lived."

"Really?"

Freya nodded excitedly. "It's just as Grandma remembers it."

"As it is now?" Mark was surprised.

"Of course. I told them about Ethan too."

"Look, Freya…" Mark put his hand over hers. "I really think you're blinded by your obsession. Leofric Farm is a ruin and Ethan, if he exists, cannot possibly be living there."

Freya pulled her hand away. "It is *not* a ruin!" she said. "And Ethan does exist! Good heavens, I've been in the house, I've drunk coffee with Ethan. It's you who's obsessed, with your idea of old houses. And Ethan – are you jealous of him?"

"Jealous, ha!" Mark leaned back, glowering at her. "Of course I'm not jealous. I'm just sick of you going on about him all the time!" He pushed back his chair and strode from the canteen.

Freya stared at his half-full mug and frowned. Damn; she really didn't want to upset Mark, but Leofric Farm – a ruin?

Two days later she was idly studying her bookings when Mark stopped.

"When you've got a moment, I've something to show you in my room."

He walked away without waiting for a reply. It was the first time he had spoken to her since their argument. It was her break - she knocked on Mark's door and, at his bidding, entered.

"Shut the door." She did so.

"Come here." Mark had spread several photographs on his desk. "Look." Mark indicated the photos and watched as she bent down.

The pictures clearly showed Leofric Farm – but not as she knew it. The walls were crumbling and where the front door should have been were the remains of a tree trunk that had crushed part of the house. The yard was littered with rubble and weeds and the shed was leaning sideways, the open door hanging precariously on one hinge.

"What on earth…" Freya's voice was a whisper. "Mark, what is this?"

"Leofric Farm." His voice softened as he watched her. "I had to do it, Freya. These are photos I took yesterday. I had to prove Leofric Farm was a ruin, shatter your obsession, I was worried about you."

"Ethan?"

"Wherever your Ethan lives, it isn't here," Mark replied.

"No!" Freya uttered a hysterical cry. "No, Mark, no…"

She turned and ran from the room, ignoring the startled girl covering for her on Reception, heading for the car park. She was in her car and away before Mark could reach her.

"Freya…" he shouted. "Stop!" But it was a useless command and, shaking his head, a worried frown on his face, he returned to his room and, quickly gathering the photos together, slipped them into his drawer.

Freya drove at breakneck speed until she came to the turning for Leofric Farm. She realised she was shaking and slowed as she turned into the lane. Almost afraid to turn the corner, she held her breath as the farm came into view.

What was Mark talking about? It looked perfectly normal. She gazed around. The apple tree was still standing, the branches bending gently in the breeze, the yard was swept, from the shed came the sound of movement. What was happening? Mark must have photographed somewhere else, surely…

She slowly climbed from the car and stood uncertainly. The door opened and Ethan stood, gazing at her.

Freya was trembling. Ethan strode across the yard and took her arm, guiding her inside. As the door closed he wrapped his arms around her and held her tightly. "What's happened?"

Pulling her into the kitchen, Freya was suddenly aware of the warmth of his embrace, the comfort, and her trembling stopped.

"It's Mark," she whispered and she felt Ethan's arms tighten.

He slipped his hand from behind her back and his finger raised her head, his eyes searching hers. And then, suddenly, he kissed her, a kiss that deepened and rocked her senses, transporting her to another world, where everything was all right.

As he let her go, Freya swayed and he guided her to a seat. Pulling his chair closer, he took her hands in his. "Now, tell me what's happened."

Somehow, through the terrifying emotion that was searing her mind; she managed a garbled explanation of the photos. She saw Ethan's lips thin angrily and his eyes bored into hers. Fear rose and her heart quickened. Clara's face slipped into her mind, as if trying to reach her…

"Why have you got a photo of Clara…?" Her voice tailed off as she looked towards the dresser. The photo was no longer there. Perhaps she had been mistaken; maybe it wasn't Clara after all?

"Clara?" He looked puzzled. "Why should I have a picture of Clara?"

"There was a photo of someone, right there." She pointed to the dresser.

Ethan shook his head and smiled gently. "I

31

don't have a photo of Clara. You've had a shock, Mark's obviously trying to upset you, take you away from me… Come here." He stood and pulled her to her feet, circling his arms around her. He kissed her hair, his hands rubbing her back gently and Freya felt herself relax. It seemed so right… Right?

"I don't understand," she whispered against his chest. "What is going on, Ethan?"

"Going on?" He laughed, holding her away from him. "Nothing's *going on*. Mark is jealous, that's all. He's trying to spoil our relationship."

"What relationship?" Freya pulled from his arms and stared up at him.

"I love you, Freya, you know that." His hand brushed her cheek. "And you love me, if you'd only admit it."

"Love you…?" Her heart somersaulted and she started to tremble. Did she love Ethan? She was attracted to him, she couldn't deny that. She loved Leofric Farm, felt at home there, but…

Sudden terror forced her from his arms. She backed away and, before he could reach for her again, she opened the door and ran across the yard to her car. Slamming the door, she locked it.

A mournful howl echoed from the shed as if he too were in agony. She swerved from the verge and turned, narrowly missing Ethan as he jumped to the side. As she careered down the lane, she glanced in the mirror. His arms stretched towards her, and she heard the sound of his voice as he shouted something. Pulling onto the main road she drove unsteadily in to a layby and, stalling the engine, she put her face in her hands and wept.

Ethan shut the door slowly. He stood, a thoughtful look on his face, and then he opened the drawer of the dresser and picked up the photograph. His fingers touched the cold face lightly. "Clara," he mused, "you thought you'd escaped me." He smiled and pushed the photo away. "But you haven't! You're back and this time I shan't let you go."

Freya returned to the desk, driving all thoughts of Ethan and Leofric Farm from her head. She apologised for her lapse and pleaded a sudden headache. Inside she felt numb, her mind refusing to acknowledge any of the previous events.

She hardly remembered the remainder of her shift, slipping to her room as soon as it was over.

Surprisingly, she slept and the next morning she wondered if the whole nightmare had been a dream. She refused to dwell on Mark's photos or Ethan, she felt weak and frightened. Ignoring the questions and emotions that imprisoned her mind, she concentrated on her work and the hotel.

She was so engrossed in stifling her inner turmoil, it was several days before she noticed that Mark was not his usual chirpy self. Looking worried and pale he approached her desk.

"Whatever's the matter, Mark?" Freya looked up, suddenly concerned, as Mark placed a sheaf of paperwork in front of her. "You look awful, are you ill?"

Mark shook his head wearily. "I don't know, Freya. I can't sleep. I'm just tired I think, but maybe I'm going down with a bug."

"Are you worried about something?"

Mark shook his head. "It's nothing like that. I keep having these awful nightmares. They seem so real, so vivid. I wake and find I'm in bed but then, every time I slip back to sleep, it's there again. It's more comfortable to stay awake!" He grinned ruefully.

"The same dream?"

"Always the same. I've had it for three nights now."

"Want to tell me about it?"

Mark looked around. There was no one in Reception.

"It's difficult to explain. It sounds so daft."

"Try me." Freya smiled encouragingly and leaned her arms on the desk.

Mark's eyes darkened. "I'm always in this orchard - I don't recognise it, and then I hear a roar and a lion is charging towards me. He's running, great hooping runs, his mane is bouncing and his jaws are open. I know he's going to attack me. His eyes – it's strange, I can see his golden eyes, glowing like embers in a fire, and they're looking directly at me." Mark shuddered. "I turn to run, but everywhere there are trees, large trees that bar my escape, every way I turn I face a tree. And then I'm against a tree trunk and I turn…"

"And?" Freya asked as Mark lapsed into silence.

"And then he pounces and I feel the pain and… and I wake up." Mark's voice is shaking. "It's daft, but I really feel as if it's happening. The dream never fades, it stays with me, haunting me."

"It sounds terrible."

"It is."

"Perhaps, now you've told me, it won't come again."

Mark shook his head. "I don't know, I just don't know. Anyway, I'd better let you get on with those bookings." He forced a smile. "See you at lunchtime?"

Freya nodded, but she watched him thoughtfully as he left. She felt an uneasiness in her mind. A lion, in an orchard? It sounded like a silly nightmare but, suddenly, a strong sense of foreboding filled her. Why should she immediately think of Leofric Farm and its orchard, and Ethan's soul-mate?

Really, she chided herself, you're getting far too fanciful. How could Leofric Farm have anything to do with a dream Mark was having? It was strange though. Three nights, Mark said, and it was three days since her confrontation with Ethan about her friendship with Mark. It was she who ought to be having the nightmares, not Mark.

And besides, she felt her stomach churn. She wasn't afraid of lions. In fact, the opposite. She stood, staring unseeing at the papers in her hand, her mind winging back to her childhood and the incident with the lion.

Waking one night, she had seen in the dim light a lion, lying by her bed, his chin resting on her duvet, his large eyes staring at her. She had stared back, wanting to reach out...

Instead, she had screamed and the lion heaved a great sigh, rose and padded out of the room. Her mother was unconvinced of course, but Freya still felt in her heart that the lion had been real and she often wondered what would have happened had she reached forward and stroked the soft mane. He never came again. Hence the 'Clara moments' as Elspeth named her daughter's flights of fancy.

She remembered a few years later, her parents took her to the Safari Park one Sunday afternoon. All went well until they drove into the lion enclosure. A lion stood, its front paws planted firmly on the verge of the road, its abundant mane glowing brown-gold in the sunbeams. Its tawny eyes stared at Freya through the window and she had an irresistible urge to leave the car and throw her arms around the lion's neck, to bury her face in the soft fur and whisper, *I'm sorry*.

It was only her mother's quick action that prevented her with the clang of the central locking. Her mother's frightened scolding caused a tantrum. Her father drove from the enclosure and, as her howling turned to hiccoughing sobs, she was led to the café. But even chocolate biscuits and ice cream couldn't appease the sadness of loss that filled her heart.

Ever since, she had felt an affinity with lions, pictures evoking a sense of bewildered longing.

A week later, as they wandered by the river, Mark pulled her down onto their favourite bench.

"What is it, Mark?" Freya asked. He looked even paler than before, and he had lost weight.

"I'm going home, Freya." Mark turned to look at her, anguish in his eyes. "I really feel quite ill and I think I need to take some time off. The manager has agreed, he's found a temporary replacement."

"But you'll come back?" Freya was shocked by the suddenness of his departure and was surprised at her own reaction. She felt tears start in her eyes and her heart plummeted. She might not love Mark as she would wish but she had grown extremely fond of him and hated the thought of life without him.

"I don't know." Mark stared across the hurrying water. "I just don't know, Freya."

"When do you go?"

"Tomorrow morning."

The walk back to The Bull was morose. Freya squeezed Mark's hand, but he hardly responded, his head bowed and his steps heavy.

The next morning Freya was up early, determined to say goodbye to Mark. He was struggling with his luggage in the hall. Without a word, she picked up a suitcase and followed him out to the car park. She watched as he stashed everything away. Slamming the boot lid he turned to her and she went willingly into his arms. He held her close for a few moments and then released her with a wry smile.

"I'll miss you, Mark." Freya's voice was husky. "And thank you for all the wonderful outings. But," she hesitated, "your photos were wrong, Mark. That wasn't Leofric Farm."

He stared at her for a moment and sighed. "Okay," was all he said.

The silence was uncomfortable.

"Perhaps…" Mark spoke at last, his eyes shadowed. "We can keep in touch?"

Freya hesitated. "Maybe."

Mark turned and slipped into the car. Freya felt a deep sadness and she reached out to touch his arm.

"You will come back?"

He looked up at her. "Hopefully. I want to, Freya." He put his hand on her arm. "I was hoping…" His eyes sought hers and then he sighed, gently closing the door.

With a brief wave, Mark drove slowly out of the car park and away. Freya walked thoughtfully back to her desk, her heart heavy.

It was her day off. The sun was shining and she decided to walk to the river. She hesitated as she picked up Clara's journal and slipped it into her bag.

She had taken it out of her drawer several times but, for some reason, had been reluctant to read it. But curiosity was plaguing her mind and she knew whatever truths the pages held, she had to know.

Settled on the bench, she reached for the journal and untied the ribbon. The river flowed peacefully below her and the meadows were quiet. Taking a deep breath, she stared at the photograph of Clara.

"Well, Clara," she whispered, "now is the time to discover your secrets." Clara's eyes stared solemnly into hers and Freya felt a rush of sadness. She would like to have known Clara, she had a feeling they were kindred spirits.

She opened the book and read the first entry:

Today, the first of September 1939, I am twenty one and war has been declared. This journal is my present from Bea. She says I must record my life and feelings. I'm not sure about that, never having thought about such a thing before. I will try. George is going mad, trying to find someone to run the farm. He is determined to join the army although, as a farmer, he is exempt. But when my brother sets his mind to something, then it usually happens. He has gone down to the village today to see a man who is passing through. He is not local but, apparently, he is looking for work. I hope he has experience in farm work otherwise it will be Bea and I doing it all! I wonder if George will remember my birthday.

Freya stared into the flowing river. She had a sudden image of Clara, a feeling Clara was there, with her, watching her reading her private thoughts. She shivered. 'Well, Clara?' she whispered. 'Should I read on?'

She flicked over several blank pages. Then came an entry that made Freya take a deep breath. Clara's words made it all too real:

My brother left today to join the army. The last few days have been unhappy ones, especially for Bea with her new baby. The infant is placid enough and sleeps well, but Bea is naturally nervous. I will help all I can. Molly is a dear little girl. We all cried when George left and he too, seemed upset. The new man, Thomas, running the farm, seems to know what he is doing. He is older than I, but not by much I think. He has a room in the village and will come every day. He is a strange man, tall and strong and, I suppose,

attractive. But I find him unnerving. He watches
me with his tawny eyes and, although he smiles, I
am somehow a little afraid of him.

Freya felt a strange sensation of timelessness. She felt Clara's fear and, somehow, it mirrored her own. Her thoughts sped briefly to Ethan and she shuddered, suddenly cold. She slammed the book shut and pushed it back into her bag. She stood up and walked quickly away.

She lay in bed that evening, staring at the ceiling. What was the mystery surrounding Clara? Why did she feel the answer lay at Leofric Farm, with Ethan? She had to return, find out the truth. But it was history, was there any need to delve any deeper? In her heart she knew that the past of Leofric was contaminating the present – her present. Somehow she and Clara were connected; with Ethan?

Should she go home and forget all about her forefathers, forget about Clara – and Ethan. She felt that would be the safest thing to do. And yet… Could she get on with her life now she had released the feelings that tied her to Ethan and Clara? No, she had to know the truth, however scary it might be. Dispel the spirits that wandered restlessly about the farm, ghosts of the past, emotions that disrupted the peace of Leofric.

Mark's face floated into her mind and she felt a wrench in her heart. She missed him. She examined the thought. He had been such good company, fun and so… normal. She could have shared the diary with him – got his down-to-earth response. She knew he was annoyed with her obsession with Leofric Farm, but he was there and, suddenly, she wanted him to come back.

She approached the farm slowly. Turning off the engine, she climbed out of the car and gently pushed the door shut. There was no sign of Ethan. First, his companion. Creeping through the gate, she crept stealthily across the yard to the shed. There was no sound. She circled to the back and the large window that looked out across the orchard. Raising herself on her toes, she looked in. The shed was empty. No sign of any animal, no dishes, no bed, nothing but dust and cobwebs.

She stepped back, her heart beating, she had been so sure...

"What are you looking for?"

She hadn't heard Ethan approach and she jumped. "Ethan!" Her voice was breathless.

"There's nothing in there." His voice was soft and his eyes searched hers.

"I thought..." She hesitated. "Daniel?"

He shook his head, a slight smile on his lips.

"Then what...?"

"Come into the house." He turned and, subdued, she followed.

She watched as he made tea and handed her a mug.

"I have a power animal," he said quietly. "But he doesn't live in the shed."

"A power animal?"

"Everyone has a guardian angel – a power greater than themselves; call it a spirit or whatever, to guide you through life, protect you – whether you recognise it or not, that force is there."

41

"And your soul-mate?"

He hesitated for a moment, his eyes searching hers as if unsure whether to divulge his secret.

"Mine? I believe I have a power animal as my guardian angel from the other-world. It is a faith founded by an ancient tribe and practised still, even in the Western world."

"An *animal*?"

"A lion."

"A lion? But the bone, the…"

"A power animal needs nurturing. I do things to please my spirit, take walks, eat food it would enjoy."

"But I heard it," Freya whispered. "It howled, I heard movement… There was something there!"

He shook his head. "If you heard Daniel, then you have the same guiding power. Have you never felt affinity with an animal in your life, an animal that seemed to be in your very soul?"

Freya caught her breath, her eyes widening. His words echoed in her heart, like some distantly whispered secret.

Ethan leaned forward, smiling into her eyes. "You have," he said softly. "And I believe it is a lion, as is Daniel."

He watched her for a moment. "That is what binds us, Freya, that is why I've come for you."

"Come for me?"

"You belong with me, you always have."

Freya shook her head, her hands trembling as she placed her mug on the floor. "I don't understand any of this, Ethan, you're frightening me."

He knelt beside her and took her hand, stroking the fingers. "We are meant to be together. It is our destiny, Clara."

"I am *not* Clara!" Freya snatched her fingers away.

"Clara is in you, Freya. I see her, feel her."

"I am not Clara," Freya repeated, her voice rising.

"You have the spirit of Clara in you. I shan't let you go away again."

"What happened to Clara? What did you do to her?" Freya's heart was thudding.

"I did nothing to her, Freya. I loved her, I tried to convince her…" He shook his head.

"Clara disappeared. Did you…?"

He frowned and his eyes grew cold. "I wouldn't harm Clara. She was foolish, stupid; but you, Freya, you understand."

She gazed at him, her thoughts in turmoil. This was Thomas. Thomas was Ethan. She shook her head – impossible! There must be some explanation.

"Thomas," she said and he stiffened. "Thomas, Ethan – who are you?"

He smiled gently. "To Clara I was Thomas; to you I am Ethan. We are both one and the same."

This was a nightmare, and yet… somewhere deep in her soul she knew he was speaking the truth and she was a pawn in his destiny, following the planned route to Hereford and Leofric Farm. She'd had no choice.

She bowed her head to her hands

"There's nothing to be afraid of. Just follow your heart."

"I have to think about this." She rose and made her way unsteadily towards the door.

"Please, Ethan," she turned, her voice

breaking, "leave me alone."

"I can't do that." He sighed and shook his head. "No, Freya, I can't. You belong to me. It's too late."

"Oh, no, it's not!" Freya felt sudden anger give her strength. She wrenched open the door and ran across the yard, turned her car clumsily and sped away. "You're nuts, Ethan, nuts!" she muttered as she gripped the steering wheel. I've had enough! I shan't come again and perhaps the apple tree will fall and ruin Leofric Farm, and take you with it."

Angrily she tooted at a motorist who overtook on the bend. "Stupid, stupid man!" she shouted through the windscreen.

Arriving back at the hotel, she prepared for her shift, her thoughts in turmoil. She'd find the truth at the farm indeed! All she'd found was more mystery, and not very nice mystery at that – power animals! Whatever next?

That evening she reached for Clara's journal again and read on:

I have neglected my journal of late. I find it rather tiresome to write in it every day when there is so much to do. What with the farm, and baby Molly, my hours are full. We miss George dreadfully and news is not good. We pray every night for his safe return.

We had a letter and form today, concerning Thomas. Apparently there is no detailed record of him on the government files. All they knew was his name, but no date of birth or any other

44

information. I gave it to Thomas when he came in for lunch. He glanced at it and pushed it into his pocket. He said he would return it, but I know he won't. He is a mystery, Thomas, and I think he will remain so.

So Clara had mysteries in her life as well, Freya mused. She turned a page.

It was Molly's first birthday today. She is growing into a lovely child and has taken her first steps. We have had an occasional letter from George, but he says very little and I wonder how long this terrible war will go on. I am trying to help on the farm as much as I can but I am uneasy about Thomas. He is pleasant and often takes a meal with us at midday, but he says nothing of his past and I am left to wonder. I gather he has a pet, his soul-mate he calls him. I think it must be a dog and I did say he could bring the animal with him if he wished. He seemed to think it would not get on well with our spaniels and was not friendly to strangers, so he declined my offer. It is the way he looks at me I find disquieting, almost as if he can read my soul and his occasional touch makes my heart jump in a most uncomfortable way. I cannot be fond of him, it would be totally unsuitable and George will be furious when he comes home. I hear Molly crying, I will go to her.

Freya re-read the entry. Thomas had a soul-mate – a soul-mate that he wouldn't bring to the farm. She felt prickles of ice run down her spine. What was going on at Leofric Farm – was history repeating itself?

She stared at the journal. Should she read on? Reluctantly, she turned the page.

Today, in the meadow with Thomas, the expected happened. I had known it would and have been trying to avoid being alone with the man. He kissed me. I tripped in the grass and when he took my arm to steady me, he didn't let go. His eyes held mine and there was no escape. I felt the inevitability of the embrace and could not resist. I cannot describe my feelings, utter abandonment to his control, an awakening in my heart that sent my pulses racing and, with desire, was fear. Finally I struggled free and ran, ran to my room to write down my emotions, although my hand is shaking and my heart still beats as if to burst from my chest. I am so afraid.

Freya's heart was thudding. Clara had expressed the feelings so eloquently that she herself had felt when Ethan kissed her. It was uncanny and very scary.

I am having the most terrible nightmares. I expect it is all the stress. We have had no news of George for a while and Bea seems exhausted. We try to keep our spirits up and Molly is such a happy child it is difficult not to laugh with her. We have shown her pictures of her daddy and hope she masters the word by the time he returns. My dreams are of capture and no escape. I am running through an orchard, chased by a lion of all things! Suddenly I am surrounded by trees, so close I cannot squeeze between them and, as I turn, I look into the jaws of the lion as it is about to pounce. Thank God, I have woken then, but I am getting afraid of going to sleep. The dream does not fade in the daylight and the fear stays with me.

Freya felt as though she was going to faint. Mark's dream. What did all this mean? Standing hurriedly, she went to the window staring out into the mellowing evening. How could Mark have had the same dream as Clara? And always – the lion! The animal that was her friend, Thomas' soul-mate? Who would protect him? But, surely, Thomas had wanted Clara, why would he harm her? Unless she had refused him... Freya's thoughts careered through her mind, confused, jumbled, frightening. She returned to the chair and stared at the journal. What other secrets did it hold? Tentatively she turned another page. A few words only:

Thomas is persistent in his attentions. He has told me I must marry him, our destiny is together. I am so befuddled by it all, I cannot think straight.

Freya shivered, her heart feeling the fear in the words. Quickly she read the next entry:

At last we have had good news. George is coming home. Bea wept and Molly joined her in howling. Such a noise! Apparently he has been wounded and in hospital but is now well enough to travel home. He will be with us in a few days, it is such a relief. I am overwhelmed with relief. Perhaps, now, we will not need Thomas on the farm and I can be left in peace. It's strange, the thought leaves an ache in my heart. But I must be free.

I have told Thomas. He said nothing at first, just stared at me. Then he replied that, when he left, I should go with him. He was most insistent and held my arm so tightly it hurt. I cried out and tried to wrench free but he pulled me closer and his eyes seemed to pierce my soul. "You will come with me, Lily!" He called me Lily. I shudder as I hear those words again in my head. I stared at him, his eyes were vacant. "Lily?" I whispered and his mouth tightened and anger blazed in his eyes. Somehow I pulled free and in my fear shouted that it could never be – I was not going with him. I ran then and reached the sanctuary of my room. I am inclined not to leave here until George returns! I have not told Bea any of my fears as I do not wish to alarm her and we needed Thomas. But now? I feel trapped and I am so afraid. I will show George my journal and he can decide what to do.

Freya turned the page, afraid for Clara.

George is home and the house is full of joy. My brother has a leg injury but, other than a limp, he seems to be in fine spirits. He does not talk about the war. He told us this morning he has dismissed Thomas with ample reward for his help. So, Thomas has gone. Why do I feel so desolate at this news? He did not even call to say goodbye. But I think maybe there is no need to show George my journal. It is over and life will go on.

I do not feel inclined to continue with my notes. This is not a happy book. I still dream of the lion, although not every night, and now Thomas stands by him, waiting. I am hoping these dreams will fade and I can dismiss Thomas from my mind but, somehow, I still feel he is near. I shall hide this journal. I cannot destroy it. If Thomas ever comes for me...

Freya flicked through the pages and nearly missed the last entries:

Thomas came back last night. He banged on the door and George had to threaten him with his rifle before he would go away. Thomas called my name over and over, I heard it all night in my sleep. I showed George my diary – he said he was sorry he hadn't shot Thomas! I smiled although I felt distraught.

George has come up with a plan. I shall go to Edinburgh, he has already spoken to a cousin that resides there and I will be welcome. I'll start a new life, find some work and banish Thomas from my thoughts. It will be hard and I am not happy at the prospect but it is for the best. George will tell no one, other than Bea of course. I will miss Molly terribly. I would like to have seen her grow up. Maybe one day...

Freya flipped through the rest of the pages but there were no more entries. She found her heart beating in sympathy and, as she shut the book, a photograph dropped to the floor. She picked it up and stared at the face before her, her hands shaking. Surely this was Ethan? She shook her head, it wasn't possible! Turning the photo over, she read: *Thomas Ethan Randle 1940*. She set the book down with shaking hands and, clutching her arms around herself, stared unseeing out of the window. Clara's Thomas was Ethan... It was true!

She needed Mark. The longing was deep in her heart and she buried her face in the pillow and wept. She couldn't cope with this alone, she needed help. Fear fed panic and her sobs became uncontrollable. Eventually, spent, she sat on the edge of her bed in despair. What was she to do? Crawling into bed, she pulled the duvet over her head and, exhausted, she slept.

Mark stayed in her mind for the next few days and then, one morning, as she manned Reception, he walked in the door.

Her heart flipped. Perhaps she was psychic, had willed him back with her thoughts!

"Mark!" She rushed from behind the desk and flung her arms around him. "How wonderful. What are you doing here, are you back?"

"Woao!" Mark laughed. "What a lovely welcome."

Pink cheeked, she stepped away. "Sorry." Her voice was husky. "I'm just so glad to see you."

"Well, that's a relief. I did wonder what sort of reception I'd get."

"Are you better?"

"Much. It was strange. As soon as I got home and rested for a couple of days, the nightmares stopped. I saw the doctor and he seemed to think it was stress."

Freya decided now was not the time to mention Clara's dream. "Are you staying?"

He nodded. "I phoned up, the temp was happy to move on, so I start work tomorrow."

"I'm so glad you're back, Mark."

Mark grinned. "I wanted to give Hereford one more try; and you."

Freya turned away, her heart hammering and sought refuge behind the desk. "Coffee later?"

"Love to." Mark picked up his case and headed towards the lift.

Freya gazed after him. Trying to make sense of her feelings, the happiness she felt at Mark's return as if, somehow, it would solve her problems. She felt as if a great weight had been lifted from her mind. If she could share all that had happened with Mark… But she didn't want to scare him away again.

"So, what's been going on while I've been away?"

Freya and Mark were sitting in the staff room at the end of her shift. Mark had been back several days and it felt as if he had never been gone.

Freya hesitated. They were so comfortable together, Mark's dreams hadn't returned, something she had been afraid of although, the thought came unbidden to her mind, Ethan didn't know Mark was back. She shuddered.

"Quite a lot." Freya kept her voice light.

"Leofric Farm?"

She nodded.

"Want to tell me about it?"

"I'm not sure…"

"A trouble shared…"

"It all seems so crazy, you'll think I'm mad."

"Try me." He placed his hand on her arm.

"I need to pop upstairs." She went before she could change her mind, returning with Clara's diary.

She began slowly, relating her visits to see Ethan; Ethan calling her Clara; Clara's journal; the photo... When she had finished her eyes were full of tears.

"Read that." She thrust the journal at Mark, who hadn't uttered a word during her outpourings.

As she reached for a handkerchief and composed herself, she heard the pages turning.

She closed her eyes and leaned back in the chair, waiting for Mark to finish reading. At last she heard a snap as he closed the book. She opened her eyes. He was staring at the photograph in his hand.

"Well?" Freya broke the tense silence.

"I don't know." Mark sounded bewildered. "It all makes sense if you believe in ghosts!" He gave a wry smile. "But Clara's dream..." He shook his head and shivered. "I've never believed in the supernatural... Did you tell Ethan about me?"

Freya nodded.

"So he wanted to get rid of me, and Clara who rejected him. It all sounds crazy!"

"I know and I don't know what to do."

"Who's Lily?"

Freya shook her head. "I thought I might Google Leofric Farm, find out its history, but I haven't found the courage yet. I've felt as if I'm going mad. I didn't know who to turn to."

"Well, now you've got me. Not that I think I

52

can help, it's all way beyond my comprehension. But I can research Leofric Farm if you like?"

"Would you, Mark? That might tell us something, explain…"

"If it can be explained!"

Mark rose and took Freya in his arms. "Don't worry, there's two of us on the case now, we'll get to the bottom of this."

Freya, reassured, said goodnight and went upstairs. She felt as if a great weight had been lifted from her shoulders, although the fear still gnawed at her mind.

It was a very worried Mark who followed her up the stairs.

It was to be two days before Mark had an afternoon off and he shut himself in his office in front of his laptop.

At the end of her shift Mark took Freya's arm. "Come with me."

He put two chairs in front of his laptop. "I've delved into the archives of The Hereford Times and found these articles. Take a deep breath, Freya, they'll shock you."

Freya glanced at him and shivered.

She concentrated on the screen as Mark scrolled to the ancient reports:

Hereford Times – Archive copies
5th January 1889
The betrothal is announced between Thomas Randle, farmer, of Leofric Farm, Herefordshire and Lily Ambrose, daughter

of Joshua and Ruth Ambrose, Manor Farm, Worcester.

20th July 1890
Carnage at Leofric Farm

Horrific violence occurred at Leofric Farm on Sunday. Lily Ambrose was on a visit with her mother to her betrothed, Thomas Randle, at Leofric Farm. Mr Randle has, on many previous occasions, incurred the wrath of local residents by his wildlife enclosure. The animal enclosed therein is dangerous and Mr Randle has been approached by law enforcement officers to question the safety of his enclosure but, as the animal has never escaped, no measures have been taken to close the said enclosure. Mr Randle obtained his pet lion as a cub. Where he came by this unusual pet has long been a subject of concern to local inhabitants. However, on Sunday, Miss Ambrose was walking in the gardens with Mr Randle when the lion sprang from behind a tree and attacked Miss Ambrose. A farmhand heard the screams and summoned help but, by the time the police and doctor arrived, Miss Ambrose could not be saved. Mr Randle himself was unhurt.

The police investigating the death of Miss Lily Ambrose ordered the lion to be shot and Mr Randle is being held responsible for her death. Many are questioning why he is allowed to remain at Leofric Farm, but investigations are still ongoing.

27th July 1890
Gruesome Act of Retribution?

In the early hours of yesterday morning the front door of Leofric Farm was violently demolished and Thomas Randle was forcibly dragged from his bed. What happened exactly is conjecture, but a young lad, hunting rabbits in the woods behind Leofric Farm came across the body of Thomas Randle swinging from a tree. Local residents deny all knowledge of the crime and Mr Joshua Ambrose states he was abed with his wife Ruth until daybreak.

September 30th 1890

Leofric Farm, the site of death and destruction, has been sold to a farmer recently moved to Herefordshire. Mr Harold Winton was farming in the Borders and is said to be delighted with his purchase and will repair the house which has been empty. He hopes the past history of Leofric Farm can now be laid to rest.

Freya stared in stunned silence at the screen. "Lily," she whispered. "Ethan."

Mark nodded. "Somehow…" His voice cracked and he cleared his throat. "Somehow, Ethan - or his spirit - has remained at Leofric Farm, searching for his Lily."

"Then came Clara, and now me," Freya's voice trembled. "Is it possible?"

Mark shrugged. "At any other time I would have said the whole story was a load of rubbish but now, I'm not so sure. It's scary!"

"What shall we do Mark?"

"We could consult someone who knows about these things… I don't know anyone, but we could find someone I expect. Remember I took those photos of Leofric Farm and you didn't believe it was a ruin?"

"It isn't."

"But it is! Somehow, when you visit, because of Ethan and his quest, you step into his world, before the storm."

Freya shook her head. "It's crazy, mad! I think I'll just go home."

"No, that's not the answer. We need to exorcise Ethan."

"Exorcise?"

"Get rid of him."

Freya gave a nervous laugh. "Oh yes, let's do that, get rid of Ethan. Honestly, Mark, you don't know him."

"Not yet!"

"He's not going to be got rid of that easily."

"Obviously not, if he's still around after a hundred odd years. Let me think about it. We'll discuss it again in the morning, at coffee break. When's your next day off?"

"The day after tomorrow."

"Right. Now go to bed and stop worrying. We'll work something out." He kissed her cheek and pushed her out of the room. "Bed, it's late."

Freya smiled wryly. 'Don't worry' indeed. What else was she to do? The more she discovered, the more frightening the situation became. She wished she'd never come to Hereford. Papa George Winton had a lot to answer for!

They discussed what action to take the following day, but Freya knew there was only one course to follow.

"I'm going to Leofric Farm," she told Mark. "I'm going to have it out with Ethan once and for all. I can't go on like this. I'll try and persuade him, or whatever he is, to leave Leofric Farm, I'm not Lily… or Clara."

"You're not going alone, it's too dangerous."

"Yes I am."

"I've got today off too. I'm taking you." Mark took her arm. "My car."

"I've got to face Ethan alone."

"You can, but I'm still taking you. I'll be there in case of problems."

Reluctantly, but with a gut feeling of relief, she let Mark propel her to his car.

As they rounded the corner of the lane, Mark let out a gasp and stopped the car. "What…?"

Freya looked at him, surprised. "What's the matter?"

"It's Leofric Farm," Mark stuttered. "It's there."

"Of course it's there," Freya snapped.

"But… it wasn't!"

Freya shook her head and put her hand on the door handle.

"Wait." Mark moved the car slowly towards the gate. "Promise you won't go inside."

Freya hesitated as she opened the door.

57

"Promise." He caught her arm, his voice fearful.

She shrugged and pulled away without replying. Slowly, she approached the door, her heart thudding. She knocked. She heard Ethan's footsteps. The door opened. He smiled.

"Freya, you've come."

"I need some answers, Ethan." She thrust the photo at him. "Thomas Ethan Randle."

He froze, his eyes shards of ice and she took a step backwards.

"Come in." He held out his hand.

She shook her head and whispered, "Lily, Clara?"

A tormented look passed across his face and he took a deep breath.

"Come in, you must come in." He lunged for her arm but she stepped back. "Freya…" His voice was pleading and she saw fear fill his eyes. "Freya, I can't let you go."

"You have to, Ethan." Freya felt his pain as he sagged before her. "You have to."

"No," he cried wildly. "No, you're mine, you're coming with me… I've waited so long…"

This time she wasn't quick enough and she screamed as his vice grip grabbed her hair. "No, Ethan." She twisted her head, groaning at the pain.

He was pulling her towards the open door. She looked beyond him and her screaming silenced.

"Oh, my God." Ethan relaxed his grip as Freya pushed past him and knelt, extending her hand. Gently, she stroked the soft mane. A low rumble emitted from the lion's throat as he nuzzled against her. She wound her arms around the lion's neck and leant her cheek against his fur, tears streaming down her face.

"I'm sorry," she sobbed. "I'm so sorry."

Ethan stood above her, a triumphant smile lighting his face. "I knew, Freya, I knew," he cried. "Now you understand, now you have to stay."

"No, she doesn't." Mark stood in the doorway, a thick plank in his hand. "Let her go, Ethan."

Freya slowly stood up, tears blurring her vision. She felt a coldness descend on her and, when she looked down, the lion's eyes met hers, sad and soulful. He turned away, his image blurring to a golden cloud. She heard his padding footsteps in the distance as they faded into silence. "No," she whispered.

Mark advanced slowly into the hall. "Come here, Freya."

"You!" Ethan took a step towards him, his eyes blazing. "I thought I'd got rid of you! Get out," he roared. "She's mine."

Ethan sprang, but Mark stepped aside, swinging the plank. Ethan let out a howl of pain and slid to the ground.

"No," Freya screamed, but Mark was dragging her through the door. The wind seared her face, battering them both as they struggled across the yard. At the gate, Freya turned, her eyes widening. She shielded her face against the gale and sleet that stung her skin.

She peered through the rain infested air. "No," she moaned, clutching Mark's arm.

He tried to pull her away but she strained from him, staring at the devastation behind her.

On the far wall of the house, the stone started

to crumble…

A gust of wind whipped through the apple tree, slamming the branches against the roof. A blackening cloud grumbled threateningly. The noise of crashing stone pierced the air as the walls of Leofric Farm slipped to the ground.

A lightening flash lit the yard eerily and caught the apple tree. The branches creaked; the old trunk battered and weary. As the rain lashed the leaves to the ground, the branches snapped and the roots of the tree gave a shuddering groan. The earth moved and the tree, defeated, toppled slowly against the house.

Splinters and twigs whipped across the yard and the door of the shed screeched open, crashing sideways as a hinge split from the frame.

"Lily!" Ethan's voice screamed in agony and then the lion roared, echoing the fear and anguish.

Freya tried to run back but Mark gripped her arm. "No, Freya. Come away."

She stumbled to the car, her vision blurred by rain and tears. Mark strapped her in. Slowly, he pulled away and drove down the lane. As they reached the corner, Freya looked back, but could see nothing through the storm. She choked back a sob as they approached the main road.

Suddenly the rain abated and a watery sun pierced the damp gloom. The roads were dry and, as Mark gathered speed, the warmth pierced Freya's icy bones and she shivered. The storm was over.

At the farm, stones and tiles crashed and splintered, branches cracked and split. Twigs were caught in the sudden whirlwind that swept around the debris and hurtled to the sky. A flash of lightening caught the black spiral as it disintegrated into mist, wafting gently towards Hereford.

Part Two – *Be wary of undying love…*

The next few days passed in a blur. Freya was unable to concentrate, her thoughts trapped at Leofric Farm. When she thought of Ethan the tears started. It was ridiculous, but she felt as if part of her soul had spiralled away with Ethan in the dark whirlwind. She was afraid to return to Leofric Farm, too emptied of emotion to work.

Mark, also, was shaken by the events at the farm and, although he tried to comfort Freya, he felt alienated. The warmth between them had cooled. He didn't understand what had happened to Freya and he was confused.

Finally, she made up her mind. She was going home. She needed time to recuperate, to decide on her future. She had a long interview with her manager. She agreed to work until a replacement could be drafted in and then she would leave.

The next day Mark called her into his office.

"I hear you're leaving. You're not coming back?"

"I don't think so, Mark."

"We need to talk about what happened. You can't run away without explaining… I was involved too, you know. I wish I hadn't been, but I can't shake off this feeling of dread. I'm scared; I don't understand what it was all about. I need to talk it through with you. I think it might help us both."

"I expect you're right." Freya sighed. The last thing she wanted was to discuss the trauma with Mark but, as he said, he had been involved and he was obviously suffering too.

They stared at each other and then Freya reached forward and placed her hand on Mark's.

"What do you want to know, Mark?"

He shrugged. "What was it all about? I mean…"

Freya sighed. How to explain? "Well," she began, "you know Leofric Farm belonged to my family and, when I found it, I saw it as it was in the past." Her words sounded lame. "You saw it in the present, a ruin. I met Ethan who, although he was real to me, wasn't real."

Mark raised his eyebrows.

"I can't explain, Mark. Maybe I'm clairvoyant like Aunt Clara, maybe my imagination changed my perception." She pressed his hand. "I just don't know, Mark."

"But I saw the farm, the storm, Ethan…"

"Perhaps you were convinced by my imagination, and your perception changed."

He shuddered. "I just want to make sense of what happened, forget the whole thing, get on with my life…"

"There is no sense in what happened, it just… did."

"And I have to accept that?"

Freya nodded. "I can't explain anything, not Leofric, not Ethan, not…" She stopped - no point in mentioning the lion; that would only make matters worse.

"I'm sorry I got you involved, Mark, truly sorry. I wouldn't have hurt you for anything. But I don't understand either, the past, the present, one affecting the other, we know so little about the paranormal."

"I don't believe in it!"

"Then I hope you can rationalise what happened and put it behind you. Get on with your life."

"I intend to." Mark stood up and stared at Freya. "I'm sorry Freya."

"Don't be. After all, you saved me in the end. If you hadn't been with me at Leofric, pulled me from Ethan…"

"Best forgotten." Mark managed a slight smile. "Perhaps one day I'll tell the children about the time I was a hero; in their bedtime fairy story."

Freya stood and brushed his cheek with her lips. "Thanks Mark. I'm so sorry…"

"I daresay I'll get over it!" He gave a rueful smile. "But I'll miss you, Freya."

Freya left his office and quietly shut the door. She felt so confused. Mark was such a dear man and she knew she'd hurt him dreadfully. She hoped that, once she had gone, he would put the episode behind him and forget her. She wished him happiness and one day he would find that – without her.

The replacement arrived at the end of the week. Freya handed over, packed her cases and walked away. She was sad as she drove from the car park. Watching Mark in the rear-view mirror, she raised her hand. This was goodbye, and they both knew it. Freya had no intention of coming back.

Elspeth welcomed Freya with a huge hug but her eyes were worried. "Aren't you well, darling? Come on in and tell me everything. Your bedroom's ready for you."

Freya followed up the stairs to her familiar room. Dumping her case on the floor, she looked around.

"Do you want to unpack now while I put the kettle on?"

"Thanks, Mum. I'll be down in a minute." Freya gave Elspeth a quick kiss and the door closed. Freya slumped onto the bed, tears starting in her eyes. She felt so sad! Blowing her nose, she stood up and resolutely opened her case. Time to settle in and then there'd be plenty of time for thought, and tears.

"So…?" Elspeth looked at Freya. "What's the matter and how long are you home for?"

Freya slowly replaced her cup on the saucer. "I'm not sure, Mum…" She hesitated. "But I'll be here for a while if that's all right?"

"Of course it's all right! But why? Are you ill?"

"Not really, Mum. I just need a break, a rest."

"Hmm." Her mother frowned, studying her daughter. "There's something you're not telling me. Is it anything to do with that Ethan you mentioned?"

Freya jumped, the mention of his name quickening her heart. "Ethan's gone, Mum."

"Ah!" Elspeth nodded, understanding dawning. "He's left and you're upset – you must have been very fond of him to come running home?"

Freya stared at the carpet. How could she possibly explain? Better her mother thought it was a broken heart that had brought Freya home. It was the simplest way at the moment. Maybe in time…

"Anyway," Elspeth picked up her cup, "I must get on with the dinner, your father will be home soon. Oh, by the way, Grandma and Grandad are coming tomorrow." With this parting news, Elspeth bustled from the table.

"Well?" Grandad Albert was sitting in the armchair, sucking his empty pipe. "Want to tell me about it, child?"

Freya twisted her hands together and stared into space. "I don't know…"

"A trouble shared…?"

Freya sighed. Would Grandad believe her if she told the truth? "It's difficult…"

Albert remained silent, leaning back, relaxed, taking an occasional slurp on his pipe. He knew there was more to the story than a broken romance; he knew Freya and he also had his suspicions about the past at Leofric Farm.

"It sounds ridiculous, you'll think I've been hallucinating, going mad…"

"Try me." His voice was gentle.

Suddenly Freya started talking. Her emotions, bottled up, spewed into the air, tales of Ethan, the diary, the storm, bursting from her in a tide of release.

There was silence when she finished, Albert studied her before removing the pipe from his mouth.

"Do you believe me?" Freya's voice shook.

"I do, lass." Albert smiled. "But I can see why you didn't tell your mother the whole story!"

Freya breathed a sigh of relief. "Thank you."

"I do believe you. I'm a bit like Clara, I feel

things. I always felt Leofric Farm held secrets from the past. Now we have them."

"But, what do I do, Grandad?"

"Do? Nothing, lass. It happened. In a way you are gifted to know the truth, but the truth can sometimes be a burden."

"But Ethan?"

"Ethan is gone. Let him go."

"But I can't forget him. I… long for him."

"That will pass. It was a traumatic experience. Try to commit it to memory. Think of the future, decide what to do next."

Freya nodded. He was right, but that didn't make it any easier. Sharing the experience had helped and the fact that Grandad believed her had lifted a great weight from her mind. At least he didn't think she was going mad! But… what now?

Days drifted by in idleness. Freya began to relax. She was beginning to feel safe, free. Every time Ethan's face filled her mind, she resolutely banished his image, immersing herself in home-life.

And then the dreams started. Freya tossed and turned, whimpering. She was in the garden at Leofrick Farm, sitting beneath the apple tree. She heard a twig snap and then, there he was, a lion, his fur glowing golden in the sunlight, his large paws padding slowly across the grass. She couldn't move, she couldn't scream as he came nearer and nearer. His face was on a level with hers and she closed her eyes, waiting…

The attack didn't happen. She felt a warm body push against hers and, when she opened her eyes, the lion was lying beside her. As she stared at him, he lifted a paw and placed it on her lap, lowering his chin so that his face rested against her. She felt warmth and comfort and an amazing joy. She cried out and put her hand on his head, stroking the soft mane. Suddenly she was crying, sobbing, and she buried her head in his fur as her body shook…

"Freya, Freya…" It was her mother, shaking her shoulders. "Wake up, Freya, you're dreaming!" Freya opened her eyes and stared at her mother, tears falling softly onto her pillow, sobs racking her body.

She sat up and sniffed, lifting the sheet to wipe her face.

"Sorry." Her voice wobbled.

"It's all right." Elspeth stroked her arm. "I heard you call out; it must have been a nightmare…" Freya shook her head and tried to focus. It had been a dream, a beautiful dream and now she had lost it. She stopped crying for her mother's sake but, as she snuggled back down beneath the duvet, her heart was heavy with longing and she wondered how she could live a normal life again. Ethan had taken that from her.

She took long walks over the cliff tops, sat and stared at the churning waves, seeking answers.

She lay in a meadow, the meadow a riot of wild flowers and grasses. She gazed upwards through the waving fronds, the faint hum of bees blending with the shush of waves on the shingle. The sky was a soft blue, puffs of white cloud wandering through her vision. She felt alone, hidden, wallowing in the feeling of freedom a secret place can evoke. Grass tickled her neck, bent against her skin and she flicked an insect exploring her face. She wished she could stay there forever, merge with the earth and let the grasses grow over her, until she no longer existed and was part of nature itself.

Freya's phone pinged with an incoming email. Cursing at the interruption, she sat up. She opened her inbox – and froze. She stared at the Subject, icicles sliding down her spine. Her hand started to shake – *Subject: Leofric Farm*. With an unsteady finger she clicked on the email:

Hi, Freya

I hope you don't mind me contacting you, but I've recently bought Leofric Farm and intend to renovate it. My family lived here in the past, before yours I believe, and I wondered if we could compare family histories sometime. I spoke to Mark at The Bull when I called in for a drink and he told me you used to work there and about your family connection to the area. I should have come to Hereford a little earlier! Anyway, perhaps you can get in touch if you feel like talking about the past.

Tom Randle

Tom…*Tom?* Freya stared through the grass, her heart hammering. What on earth was going on? Bur her thoughts were chaotic, swimming in a dark haze of fear. She took the cliff path to the beach, skittering over stones, her head buzzing. She needed to speak to Mark.

She phoned Mark as she reached the sand, watching the gentle waves rippling slowly up the beach.

"Mark, it's Freya."

"Oh… Hi Freya."

"Have you spoken to Tom Randle?"

There was a pause. "Yes, he came in for a drink last night, said he'd bought Leofric Farm."

"What, umm, what did he look like?"

"He was real!" Mark gave a chuckle. "I must admit I was startled when he came in, I thought it was Ethan returned, but he was younger, late twenties? And, although he resembled Ethan, he was certainly no ghost. A very human chap in fact. We had a long chat after I'd got over the shock!"

"Did you tell him…?"

"Of course not! He said he was a property developer. He's been doing up a cottage in Shropshire and heard about Leofric Farm being up for sale. He knew it had been his family home at some time in the past. He made an offer and it was accepted. No one else seemed very interested."

"I'm not surprised!"

"Anyway, he seemed perfectly normal and very pleasant, so don't worry, Freya. I shan't say a word about what happened. In fact I've already decided I was hallucinating, carried along on the tide of hysteria and that the whole episode was pure imagination."

"Good," Freya said. "I'm glad to hear it. Only I got an email from Tom and I was a bit spooked."

"Don't worry, Freya, Tom's no problem. Up to

you whether you talk to him or not, of course, but good luck whatever you do. Gotta go, in the middle of training my replacement. I'm transferring up North, nearer home. The opportunity came up and it seemed sensible to take it."

"I hope it works out well, Mark, and thanks. I feel better now. Good luck to you, too."

Freya closed her phone with a snap and walked briskly home, shaking off the shadows of foreboding that were clinging to the edge of her mind.

It was several weeks before Freya found the courage to return. She had taken a job in a café on the beach run by her friend, Laura. At least she was contributing to her prolonged stay at home but, try as she might, she was unable to settle and she knew the restlessness would remain until she faced her demons.

When the café was quiet at the end of September, she made a decision. She had to return to Leofric Farm, meet Tom. He hadn't emailed her again, nor had she replied; but neither had she deleted his message.

Telling her mother she was going to visit some friends, she booked into a guest house. She decided not to stay in Hereford, instead she chose Leominster, a small market town nearby and, she realised, closer to Leofric Farm. The drive was long and tedious and Freya nearly turned back, but some force kept her travelling. She booked into the guest house late in the evening. Tired, she crept into bed.

She found sleep difficult and lay awake

wondering what on earth had possessed her to return, her stomach churning at the thought of facing Leofric Farm in the morning. Eventually, she slept, but it was a restless sleep filled with disturbing dreams that dissipated with the morning light.

It wasn't until next morning, as she wandered around the old town with its black and white buildings overhanging the narrow streets that the name 'Leominster' registered. She was standing outside Grange Court, a 17th century market house, and her eyes were fixed on the large stone lions adorning the main entrance. 'Leo-minster' she whispered to herself. Would she always be haunted by lions?

She couldn't dawdle any longer. Bracing herself, she drove until she came to the lane. Taking a deep breath, she turned in and followed the familiar route. As Leofric Farm came into view she gasped out loud, her heart hammering. Pulling up once again in the layby, she stared. The house was being rebuilt. She could see where the old stone was melding with new. Shaking, she scrambled out of the car and crossed the lane.

The stone wall had gone. Instead, a privet hedge had been planted. Across the yard the shed had been demolished and a large caravan stood in its place.

Bewildered, she unlatched the gate. The door of the caravan opened and Freya let out a cry. At first glance she saw Ethan but, as he approached, she realised that, although he looked similar - frighteningly similar - his facial features were softer, welcoming.

"Hi, are you lost?"

Freya felt hysteria bubble as she gazed into his smiling eyes. Had she stepped back in time, again?

"I'm Freya, you emailed me."

"Good grief, Freya, come in. You've taken me by surprise!"

She followed him through the door, hesitating as she stared at the growing walls of Leofric Farm.

"You should have told me you were coming, I'd have bought a cake!" Tom laughed.

"It was a spur of the moment decision, I thought I'd visit some friends in Hereford and it seemed churlish not to call and see you."

"I'm glad you did." Tom was filling the kettle. "I'm intrigued by the history of Leofric. I've researched my family, but your family was here for many years and there's not a lot in the archives."

"I don't think we did anything spectacular enough to be recorded!" Freya laughed. "But I did learn quite a few details from my grandmother."

"I'm trying to rebuild the house as it was before. I dug up old plans and I'm using stone from the outer walls, although there wasn't a lot left. In the meantime, I'm camping on site. Coffee?"

"Please, milk no sugar," she replied automatically.

"Now," he sat opposite her, "tell me about your family history. Perhaps we're related?"

"I don't think so." Freya took a sip of her drink and stared at Tom. He was uncannily like Ethan, and yet different. "My great, great-grandfather,

Harold Winton, bought Leofric in 1890. I believe your family was here before then?"

Tom nodded. "Leofric was originally built by the Randles, centuries ago. The last Randle came to an infamous end and that must have been when your family moved in."

Freya felt a shiver pass through her. Infamous end indeed! She still had a copy of the archive entries, inside Clara's diary, tucked in the bottom of her case. She thought about showing it to Tom… not yet, the time wasn't right.

"How come you bought it?" Freya asked.

Tom sat back. "I've always been fascinated by tales of the family history and determined to find Leofric one day. I work for myself, I'm a property developer, and I had a commission in Shropshire. While I was in the area I found the farm and, to my surprise, it was up for sale. The farmer was selling the house and orchard as one lot, the idea being that planning permission would be easy as part of the walls still remained. I think he was finding things financially difficult and this seemed an ideal answer.

Anyway, I thought about it and then, 'Why not?' I had no ties, I loved the area and something in the ruins seemed to be calling me. Fate really!" He grinned.

"And so Leofric is restored to a Randle."

"Exactly! It's hard work but worth it. There's still a lot to do, obviously. I think I've got the drawings right. There were still base walls left, so the downstairs rooms are laid out. Perhaps you can take a look and see what you think? Oh, and I must plant an apple tree."

Freya slopped her drink.

"I've got an old picture of how the farm used to look. It had a beautiful apple tree in the corner of the lawn."

"Don't," Freya said. Then, seeing the look of bewilderment on Tom's face added, "It would grow and make the house very dark; be dangerous in a storm."

"We'll see." Tom was studying her and Freya thought he must think her mad!

"Sorry, it was the shock of seeing the house being rebuilt, and you here."

"A nice shock I hope?"

She stared at him for a moment. How did she really feel? Mixed emotions churned in her head and she found her hand was shaking as she replaced her cup.

"Where are you staying, Hereford?"

"No, Leominster." Freya grinned wryly. "There seem to be lions everywhere in this part of the county."

"All the legends relate to lions. You should look them up sometime, fascinating."

"Oh?"

"Well, Earl Leofric who lived in Saxon times owned most of the land, perhaps even this farm. And then there's the tale of the monk, Edfrith, and his encounter with a lion that bought peace to the waring locals…"

"Really?"

Tom nodded. "Leominster is an ancient town, famous initially for its wool, *Lemster Ore.* There are books on local folklore; I won't bore you with details now."

"Hmm, lions."

Tom laughed. "I haven't seen any real ones

yet, but I'll let you know! Are you staying awhile?"

"I'm not sure, a couple of days anyway."

"Then you must let me take you out for a meal. How about tomorrow night? Do you like Indian? Leominster has several good Indian restaurants."

"Sounds lovely, and modern enough to chase the lions away!"

"Right, give me your mobile number and I'll ring you in the morning."

Freya rose. "Thanks, Tom. I'm glad I came back."

"So am I." Their eyes met for a moment and Freya felt the same spark ignite that she had felt with Ethan. Hurriedly she turned away and left, driving her car in a daze, her thoughts in turmoil.

She went for a long walk by the river in the late afternoon, the sun slanting across the rippling water and felt her mind calm as she heard the soft call of pigeons and felt the gentle breeze whisper against her cheeks.

There was nothing odd about Tom, she knew that but, all the same, it was unsettling, his resurrection of Leofric Farm and, she had to admit, the kindling of feelings that Ethan had aroused. The sensible thing was to go home and get on with her life. The sensible thing...

Sighing she returned to the guest house and read until she was tired enough to sleep.

Tom tossed restlessly in his bed. Seeing Freya had sparked a yearning in his mind... for what? In the shadows of his mind images floated, drifted, clarifying in Freya's face, and the words 'She has come home' whispered in the dark recesses of his memory. As he slipped into an uneasy sleep, 'She has come home…' became a soft chant until sleep finally brought peace.

The call came from Tom mid-morning. She was exploring the quaint streets, seeing lions on every wall and smiling wryly to herself. Lion country! They arranged to meet at seven. Walking into the Grange, she sat on a bench overlooking the children's play area. It was quiet, school had resumed for the winter term, but the sun was pleasantly warm.

Should she stay? She could work and find accommodation, watch Leofric being rebuilt, get to know Tom. Was that wise? Her heart urged her to stay, but her head admonished her - it was dangerous, foolish - remember Ethan? As if she could forget him!

"So," Tom snapped a poppadum and dipped it, "what do you know about the history of Leofric Farm?"

"Well…" Freya hesitated, unsure how much to disclose. "I've read the stories in the paper's archive…

Tom was looking thoughtful. "About Ethan and his dangerous lion!"

Freya nodded.

"Of course," Tom continued, "if it really was a lion; or just a large dog. It seems highly unlikely that he would have a lion as a pet. Anyway, whatever it was, the vigilantes punished him for his fiancée's death. A gruesome end!"

Freya leaned back as the waiter brought an array of dishes on hot-plates. They both started spooning the deliciously smelling food onto their plates. Neither spoke for a few minutes. Freya was thinking of the lion and memories flooded her mind. She shuddered.

"I'm sure some of these old tales are exaggerated." Tom laughed. "Still, it makes fascinating history."

Freya agreed, enjoying the food. Now was not the time for revelations. She didn't know Tom well enough. Besides, would he believe her? She almost choked on her rice at his next words.

"It's strange," Tom was stirring his food, "after I'd started on the renovations and read the archives I had the strangest dream."

"Oh?"

"I was in the farm yard and there was this lion. He just walked out of the shed and towards me. I stroked his back, as I would a dog, and he rubbed himself against me and then walked slowly into the house."

Tom chuckled. "Obviously the articles had stuck in my mind; but he wasn't at all fierce. In fact, in my dream, it seemed perfectly natural that he should be there!"

Freya concentrated on her meal, her heart hammering. Tom had dreamed of a docile lion. Surely it was coincidence? Just his mind reacting to the old stories?

"How long are you staying?"

Freya made an instant decision. She wasn't ready yet to face Leofric, Tom and his lion dreams. Memories of Ethan were too raw. "I have to go home tomorrow," she said, smiling to reassure his anxious look. "I'm living at home now and I've got a job. I just took a few days off to visit friends, and you of course."

"You'll come back?" Tom was watching her intently.

"I'll visit again," Freya promised. "Possibly next year when Leofric is finished. I should like to see it fully restored."

"Shall I keep you updated by email?" Tom was persistent.

Freya stared at him for a moment. What harm could emails do? Besides, she was curious.

"Thanks, yes. When do you hope to finish building?"

Tom smiled and leaned back as the waiter removed the plates. "Well, it's taken a while to get the permissions sorted, building regulations and, of course, it's listed. On top of that we've had to put in foundations, no such thing when the old house was built! But we're on top of the paperwork and, so far, everything has been approved. I would like to move in by this time next year. Decorating and finishing off can be done when I'm living there.

I've found a very good firm of local builders and I think I can trust them to take care of everything. I still have to work and that means I won't always be around but, hopefully, next summer will see Leofric Farm taking shape."

"Lions and all?" Freya laughed.

"If there's a lion to be found I'll rebuild the shed." Tom was teasing but Freya felt a tremor of premonition pass through her mind.

Tom felt a strange anguish as Freya closed the door of the guest house. He couldn't lose her now. He knew he loved her... but he hardly knew her! This obsession was ridiculous! With a sigh he returned to Leofric and stood gazing at the climbing walls. Was he doing the right thing? For a moment doubt shadowed his thoughts. Did he really belong here or was it the past that drew him back and Ethan? Who was this ancient relative who seemed to dominate his dreams? Ethan and Freya, the two were linked he was sure. Perhaps it would be safer to walk away...

It was with a mixture of regret and relief that Freya set off for home next morning. Far from settling ghosts, her visit had created more questions, more uncertainties and her attraction to Tom was her biggest worry. Tom was dangerous, normal or not, and she didn't want to become embroiled in the clutches of Leofric Farm again. No, better she settle at home and get on with her life until she decided what she wanted to do. Her parents were happy to have her home, she had a job; that, for now, was all she needed. Her future could sort itself out.

Despite her serious conversation with herself she couldn't quench the feeling of foreboding that haunted her mind.

Freya settled into a routine at home. The café was busy enough with local customers for her to continue working there. But her mind was far from at peace and, one afternoon when sitting with Grandad Albert after dinner, she found herself telling him about her visit to Leofric Farm and Tom.

Albert sucked on his pipe and studied her thoughtfully. "So," he said eventually, "this young Tom has got under your skin!"

Freya blushed. "I don't know." She stared at her fingers as she twisted them in her lap. "I just don't know what's going on, Grandad."

"He sounds sane enough," Albert took a puff, "a Randle and a Winton... hmm, interesting."

"Really, Grandad!" Freya laughed. "You can't think that Tom and I...?"

"Why not? The circle of life..."

"Yes, but..." Freya felt her heart hammering. "Me, Leofric Farm? Far too spooky!" She shuddered.

"You can't fight fate, lass."

"Try telling that to Grandma Molly and Mum, they'll think you've gone mad."

"They already do!"

Freya thought about the conversation as she set off for work next morning. Tom and herself? Never! But the seed remained and, although she made every effort to smother her thoughts, her dreams at night invaded her peace.

It was Christmas before her fragile mind was again disturbed by an email:

Happy Christmas, Freya. Just thought I'd keep you up to date on renovations. Leofric Farm is taking shape and, so far, the weather has been kind and the builders are on schedule. They found something fascinating when they took down part of an inside wall – a photograph in a silver frame. The silver is tarnished and the glass broken, but the photo itself is intact. Amazing! I'm attaching a copy in case you recognise the young lady, maybe one of your family?

81

Anyway, I'd be interested to find out, she's very pretty! I hope you're enjoying being with your parents and that you have a wonderful Christmas. I, too, shall be going back to my family for the festivities and I've some work lined up for the New Year which is good.

I enjoyed meeting you and hope to see you again soon? Please keep in touch. Merry Christmas, Tom

Freya slumped down onto a chair and stared at the screen. Her finger hovered over the attachment, but she found she was shaking and pulled away. She would have to reply to Tom, perhaps she'd do that first. After several attempts her reply was brief:

Happy Christmas to you too, Tom. Glad to hear that Leofric is progressing. Everything is fine here and thanks for the good wishes, Freya

She hesitated and then clicked 'send'. Then she opened the attachment and her heart almost stopped. It was the photo of Clara, the photo that had been on Ethan's dresser on her visit to Leofric, the photo that Ethan had later denied all knowledge of.

Aunt Clara, psychic Aunt Clara, whose diary was hidden upstairs in the bottom of her suitcase. She closed her pad. Thrusting the email and its contents to the back of her mind she went to help her mother with the Christmas preparations. She couldn't think clearly, couldn't focus on the implications. She would later, when her mind had cleared and, feeling panic hovering, she burst into the kitchen.

It was early Spring when she heard from Tom again. She had pushed the memory of the photo to the back of her mind, determined to get on with her life. New Year's Resolution: *I will not think of Tom and Leofric Farm!* She was doing reasonably well, even if she couldn't control her dreams or wandering thoughts as she surfaced from sleep.

It was another email that challenged her resolution:

Hi Freya

I'm going to be in Cornwall, looking at a property in a few days. Can I call and see you? Then I can update you on progress at Leofric.

Please, Tom

Freya felt a peculiar sense of defeat. She went to find her mother and read out Tom's email.

"Why, he must stay here of course." Elspeth was delighted." We've the spare bedroom and, if he's bought Leofric Farm, then he's almost part of the family! I must let Grandma know."

"Mum!" Freya was alarmed at her mother's enthusiasm. Family indeed! "He might not want to stay with us."

"Then ask him, now." Her mother returned to the sink, humming cheerfully.

With a sigh of resignation, Freya clicked reply.

Tom, what a surprise! Mum would be delighted if you could stay with us, she wants to hear all about Leofric, so do the Grandparents (she hoped that might put him off) *so let me know what you want to do. Freya*

The answer was immediate:

That's wonderful of your Mum, Freya and I'd like to accept. It would be a pleasure to meet your family and discuss Leofric. Your grandparents can probably relate more of the history. Send me your address so I know where I'm coming to! I'll let you know when I'm sure, but I think it will probably be next Monday. Thanks, Tom

'Monday,' Freya muttered. Four days to compose herself. The café didn't open on a Monday this early in the season so she had no reasonable excuse not to be there when he arrived. Frowning, she went to tell her mother.

It was an agitated four days for Freya. She tried to ignore the thoughts that circled her mind, calm herself and think rationally, but she couldn't rid herself of the feeling of impending doom. Unless she ran away, she could see no resolution other than to let fate take over.

Freya woke early on Monday morning and lay staring at the ceiling. Today Tom was coming and, not for the first time, she felt totally out of control of her life. She dressed reluctantly. Tom wasn't due until the afternoon so, after helping her mother with breakfast, she took a long walk through the meadows on the cliff top, watching the churning sea that echoed the state of her mind.

She felt reasonably calm when she returned and was taken completely unawares as she entered the kitchen. "Put the kettle on, Mum, I'm…" She broke off in mid-sentence. There, seated at the table, mug in hand, was a grinning Tom.

"Tom!" Freya felt the heat rise in her cheeks and her heart thudded.

"Come and sit down, Freya, don't stand there gawping!" Elspeth bustled about, reaching for another mug. "Tom set off early and we've had a long chat." Her mother was beaming and Freya wondered what they'd been talking about.

Shaking slightly, she collected her thoughts and sat down. "Sorry, Tom, I should have been here to welcome you," she said. "I wasn't expecting you this early. I've been along the cliffs, the sea's quite wild today but it's not too cold." She was aware she was blathering and shut up.

"That's okay, Freya, I've been getting to know your mother and we can catch up on news when I've unpacked."

"Fine. How's Leofric?"

"Coming on well. I was just telling your Mum, if the weather stays kind, I'm hoping to move in by the end of the summer. It's really taking shape now. I've brought some photos, you'll hardly recognise the place."

"I'd like to see them." Freya forced a smile. "Get yourself sorted and then you can show me."

"I'm just preparing a snack lunch," Elspeth said. "It'll be ready by the time you've unpacked,

Tom, and then you two youngsters can chat all afternoon."

Freya smiled weakly, her mind in turmoil.

They sat in the front room, on the settee, and Freya was aware of Tom's thigh against hers. The photos were good and she felt her heart constrict as she watched Leofric Farm coming back to life.

"Oh, Tom, it's going to be wonderful!" She felt a sudden longing to be there as she watched the walls rise and the house begin to resemble her memories.

"You must come and visit, Freya."

"Yes... yes I think I must."

She was staring at the final picture when Tom startled her out of her reverie. "I gather you left Hereford because of a broken romance?"

Freya mentally groaned. Her mother had been gossiping!

"Not exactly!" Freya was thoughtful. "Shall we say an unfortunate experience?" She smiled. "It was a long time ago."

"Unfortunate enough to make you want to come home."

Freya nodded. "But I'm happy at home now, so there's no problem."

"Oh?"

"I'll tell you about it sometime, Tom."

"I'll hold you to that! I'm rather tired after the journey today anyway, but perhaps tomorrow we can have a real talk?"

Freya took a deep breath. "The Grandparents are coming this evening, Tom. They're dying to meet you."

"I'm sure we've got a lot of history to talk about. I'll look forward to that. In the meantime,

I've some notes to make for work. I'll see you later and then, tomorrow, I really do need to talk to you." His face was serious.

"Fine, Tom, tomorrow it is." Freya smiled lightly but her heart was turning somersaults. Was now the time?

"Well, Ethan," she whispered as she slipped into slumber that night. "Is it time?"

Grandma Molly was thrilled to talk to Tom about Leofric Farm.

"I was born there, you know." She leaned forward as they sat in easy chairs after dinner. "I loved the place, but I went on holiday and met Albert and the rest, as they say, is history!" She sat back and smiled. "I've had a very happy life in Cornwall, no regrets! But I've often thought about Leofric Farm and when Freya went to Hereford and found the old place... well! And now you, a Randle, are bringing it back to life!"

Tom laughed. "It seems like fate somehow. As soon as I saw the farm I felt an immediate familiarity. It's almost as if it's been waiting for me. It's a shame it's had to wait so long, it was in very bad shape and there's still a lot to do!"

"I imagine there must be. It was sold after Papa George died, although Freya didn't seem to think it had suffered much. She actually visited..." She stared at Tom thoughtfully.

"So I gather. She told me about her job in Hereford."

The door opened and Grandad Albert carried in steaming mugs of coffee.

"Albert, Tom was just telling me about Leofric Farm. Apparently it's quite a ruin, but I thought

Freya said…"

"Coffee," Albert interrupted. "Yes, well, I imagine there are building regulations that have to be satisfied before you can start any alterations?"

"Yes, indeed. The paperwork is horrendous!" Tom sighed. "But most of that is done and passed, thank goodness, and we've started on the actual rebuild."

Albert nodded. "Do you know your family history? The last Randle to own Leofric was Ethan, I believe?" Albert was watching Tom closely. Molly looked startled, but before she could say anything, Elspeth poked her head round the door: "Mum, you said you wanted to walk to the shop with me?"

Molly eased herself from the chair and trotted towards the door. "I'll leave you two to work out relationships!" She laughed. "It all gets too complicated for me!"

The door closed behind her.

"I'm not sure of the exact connection." Tom looked thoughtful. "From reading the archives I gather Ethan came to a rather gruesome end, his whole story sounds rather far-fetched! I know he didn't have any children but he did have brothers. I imagine one of them is my great, great something or other."

Albert nodded. "Yes, I heard about the fate of Ethan, not sure what happened to his lion though!" He laughed.

Tom looked startled.

"Freya looked up the archives too." Albert realised he had said too much. "She found Leofric and it fascinated her, so she dug around on the Internet. Modern technology!"

"Ah, I see. Well, anyway, I intend to trace my family tree when I have time, see exactly how I'm connected to the infamous Ethan Randle."

Albert concentrated on lighting his pipe. "Freya came home engrossed in her find," Albert said carefully. "I think she found out more than she intended and it played on her mind for a while." He watched Tom. "She found it an … emotional experience, finding Leofric after all Molly's tales of growing up there with Papa George and his sister, Clara."

"She told me about Clara when we met in Hereford. Psychic, wasn't she?"

"So it's said."

"Well I think, as our pasts are so intertwined with Leofric Farm, we must discover the truth together!"

Albert sighed. "I expect you two youngsters will do that. The truth has a habit of presenting itself whether you want it to or not."

Tom looked at Albert curiously. "You don't think it's a good idea to uncover the past?"

"We don't always have a choice in such matters."

Tom stared at him, confused.

"Anyway," Albert puffed on his pipe and smiled at Tom, "it will give you both something to do with your time."

"As if we've time to spare!" Tom replied ruefully.

"You'll find it. How long are you staying?"

"Only a couple more days. I'm looking at a renovation prospect a few miles from here, but I have a feeling it won't be suitable. It was an excuse to come to Cornwall actually," Tom confessed, colour flushing his cheeks.

"To see Freya?"

"Do you mind?"

Albert studied him for a moment. "As long as she doesn't get hurt again," Albert said quietly.

"I wouldn't hurt Freya."

"No, Tom, I don't think you would. Now, would you like to take a walk around the garden? I'm supposed to get some exercise. It's a bit blowy out there, but not cold."

"Delighted." Tom jumped up and helped Albert to his feet. "Let's go."

When Freya woke next morning and remembered Tom, she knew it was time. Slipping the diary in her bag she went down for breakfast.

"Tom's already gone for a walk," Elspeth informed her. "He was up early, but he said he'd meet you on the beach at ten thirty."

He was waiting for her, his face breaking into a smile as she approached. He kissed her gently on the cheek.

"I'm glad you came." He took her hand and they wandered along the damp sand.

Freya laughed. "Did you think I wouldn't?"

"Not really, but nothing is certain." He was gazing across the sea to the outline of mountains on the horizon.

They came to a bench, stacked against the cliff edge. Sitting gently on the paint-stripped wood, there was silence, both lost in thoughts.

"Tom," Freya spoke hesitantly, "there's something you should see."

90

"Oh?"

Freya clasped Clara's diary in her hands. "Do you remember you asked me about a photo you found at Leofric?"

"You never replied."

"It was of my Great Aunt Clara." She caressed the faded notebook and then offered it to him. "This is her diary."

"You want me to read it?"

She nodded. "I think it's time, it explains a lot of things."

Tom looked uncertain and gingerly opened the first page. He soon became absorbed and Freya watched his expressions change as he read.

Finally he let out a huge sigh and closed the last page. "Wow!" He stared at her. "How long have you had this?"

"My Grandmother gave it me after I found Leofric. I recognised the farm although, apparently, I'd never been there, and... other things happened."

"Such as?"

Should she tell him? Her heart was racing. Only Grandad Albert knew the truth, could she trust this man who was linked to Ethan?

"I met Ethan." she said abruptly.

"You what?"

Freya half-smiled at his look. "You probably don't believe me."

"I think you'd better tell me what you're talking about. You've gone too far to hold anything back now."

That was true. Freya gazed at the waves and began slowly; her arrival at Leofric Farm, the recognition and the consequences of her discovery. It seemed to take a long while. Not once did she look at Tom.

There was silence until finally she could stand the tense atmosphere no longer.

"Well?" She turned. He was watching her thoughtfully. "Do you believe me?"

"After reading the diary, I think I do. And it would explain…"

"Explain what?"

"Feelings that I sometimes get at Leofric; as if I'm not alone, as if someone's watching me. And, as we build, the whole house becomes familiar, yet I never saw it before either. But it feels like… home; as if I belong there."

Freya stared at him. His reaction scared her for the same reason her feelings about Leofric scared her. It was as if Ethan had taken over her life, lured her to Leofric, and then, defeated, had lured Tom to Leofric Farm – for her! Ethan was never going to let her go.

"The lion business is weird too," Tom continued. "I'm forever dreaming about the damn thing. I even thought I saw one once!" He laughed, embarrassed.

"Oh, Tom, what *are* we going to do?"

"Do as Ethan wants?" He grinned as he leaned towards her and, before she could protest, he kissed her full on the lips. For a second neither breathed, then Freya found herself responding with an ardour that surprised her. Their kiss deepened as his arms drew her closer and time spun as the waves on the shore dulled to a whisper.

"Oh, my goodness!" Freya was shaking when she finally gasped for air. "Oh, Tom, oh heck!"

And, as she gazed into his eyes, her heart somersaulted. It was Ethan gazing back at her, triumph sparking.

"Well," Tom laughed shakily, "Ethan or not, I think we ought to consider seeing more of one another."

Freya smiled, trying to lighten the mood and quell her racing fear. "As you say, perhaps we ought to meet more often!"

They grinned at one another and started chasing across the sand, arriving breathless at the beach café.

"Coffee?" Tom held open the door.

"I think I could do with something stronger." Freya laughed. "But coffee will do for now."

As they sat in a window seat, steam rising from their mugs, Freya knew her future had been decided and there was nothing she could do to stop fate.

As Tom travelled back to Leofric he thought about Freya's revelations and felt a great weight lift from his mind. Suddenly he understood; and he believed every word that Freya had uttered. Now, it all made sense.

'Well, Ethan, I guess you win after all!'

Over the next few months Tom and Freya kept in touch with phone calls and emails, pictures of Leofric rising from the ruins inspiring her imagination. Freya felt her fears slipping away. Leofric looked so normal, so beautiful and she longed to see Tom again.

When she finally decided, after several pleas

from Tom, to go and see him, she booked into the guest house in Leominster again, arriving late on the Saturday. Promising to call on Tom the next day, she went to bed and slipped into an exhausted sleep.

She awoke, her heart pounding, for a moment wondering where she was. Re-orientating herself, her heart beat slowed but her mind was full of dreams. Ethan – Ethan had appeared in her dream, he was smiling and he whispered, *"I knew you'd come back to me."* And, instead of the usual horror, she had felt immense joy.

Shaking, she pulled the covers over her and snuggled beneath the duvet, trying to clear the image from her mind. Eventually she fell into a dreamless sleep and awoke refreshed, the dream hovering in the shadows of her memory.

Freya walked through the gate and stopped for a moment, eyes drinking in the house. There was no longer any fear attached to Leofric Farm, the opposite if anything. The nightmare had gone, Ethan with it, and she sometimes wondered if she had, after all, imagined the whole episode.

Whatever evil had happened in the past had no place at Leofric in the hands of Tom. It seemed absolutely right that the farm should revert to a Randle, absolutely right that Tom had rebuilt the house into a warm and loving home; she just wondered, in the back of her mind, if she dared hope fate had brought her back to stay…

Shaking off her reverie she walked towards the door – and then stopped with a sharp intake of breath. On either side of the front door posts was a large stone lion, lions that looked at her with blank eyes, watching as she approached. The door swung open.

"Hi." It was Tom. "What do you think?" Freya was standing motionless, mesmerised. "My latest acquisition. I went to a scrap yard and there they were, staring at me, begging for a home. They seem just right for Leofric, don't you think?"

"Umm, yes." Freya's voice cracked and she cleared her throat. "Perfect." She tore her eyes away and smiled at Tom. "Were there lions here before…?"

Tom shook his head. "No, but lions seem to feature in our history… and I couldn't resist them! Come in, I've baked a cake."

Freya laughed and the tension lifted.

Freya gazed in wonder as Tom showed her round. The rooms were as she remembered, but brighter, friendly, homely. She liked what he'd done. Leofric was now a home and she knew she belonged there. She let out a sigh and settled in a comfortable chair in the kitchen as Tom filled the kettle.

"Well," he had his back to her, "what do you think?"

"It's lovely," Freya replied. "Really lovely."

"Good, I'm glad you approve." He placed a steaming mug at her side and proceeded to cut her a wedge of delicious looking sponge.

"Did you really make this?" Freya asked as she took a bite of the fragrant cake.

Tom grinned. "Well, it is homemade…"

"Ah, I see!"

They laughed and sat in comfortable silence.

"Have you thought about coming back?" Tom finally asked.

Freya nodded. "A lot."

"And…?"

"I'm seriously considering it."

"Good. How about a short stay to start with. There's a spare bedroom," he added hurriedly as Freya coloured.

"Maybe a few days." Freya studied him thoughtfully. "I'm due some time off, perhaps it would be a good idea…"

"Splendid!" Tom looked thrilled. "Just let me know when you're coming and I'll get everything prepared. I'm working from here for the next few weeks, some new plans to design, so whenever suits you."

"I don't want to interfere with your work."

"It won't. I'm due a break too, I haven't stopped since I last saw you and I'm nearly up to date on projects at the moment."

"In that case…" Freya stood up.

"Do you have to go back today?"

Freya nodded. "I'm due back at work tomorrow, I can't let them down. Besides, I have a lot to think about."

Tom laughed and moved towards her. "Then let me give you something else to think about!"

His voice was husky as he pulled her into his arms, his lips warm and hungry. Freya response was immediate and she felt herself relax in his embrace. She loved Tom, there was no doubt in her mind. She belonged with him and she would be coming back.

Tom felt a surge of triumph as he watched Freya leave. She was coming home.

It was midsummer before Freya returned. She had been waiting, poring over details as Tom recounted every improvement in constant emails.

Freya, come and stay, please. The inside is complete but the house needs a woman's touch to make it feel homely. Leofric needs you!

See you soon, I hope, Tom

Freya took a deep breath. Decision time and she felt a surge of excitement. The fear had all but dissipated and, other than the night-time whisperings from Ethan which now seemed comforting rather than scary, she knew she would return.

She had already warned Laura that she would be leaving the café. Laura understood and had employed several students as she usually did during the summer months, so she wished Freya good luck and Freya made plans to return to Leofric Farm.

Her mother had mixed reactions. She would miss Freya. Elspeth had liked Tom but it was with some trepidation that she kissed Freya a fond farewell and watched until the car became a cloud of distant dust.

Freya pulled into the yard at Leofric Farm and heaved a sigh of relief. It had been a long journey and she had found it difficult to quell her anxiety. Was she doing the right thing?

The door opened and Tom walked towards her. As soon as she saw him her misgivings faded. She opened the door.

"Are you lost?" he asked teasingly.

"No, not anymore," she replied with a smile.

He welcomed her with a kiss and, taking her case, led the way into the farmhouse.

She snuggled beneath the cosy duvet and fell instantly asleep.

She dreamed she awoke and heard a movement. Leaning over the edge of the bed, she saw a lion stretched out on the carpet, his soft tawny eyes gazing at her.

This time she did not scream but, leaning over, she stroked her hand down his mane. He sighed and lay still, his head on his paws, closing his eyes, as she swept her fingers through his fur.

As she slipped back into sleep a vision of Ethan appeared. He sat on her bedside, his eyes full of love as his gentle fingers brushed the hair from her face. He leaned closer and whispered,

At last you have come home to me, my darling...

* * * * * * * * * *

13 months later

She sat on the grass, leaning against the young apple tree, the warm sun brushing her face, her hands resting lightly on her stomach and she smiled at the life growing beneath her fingers.

She was awoken by a heaviness on her lap and a softness brushing against her bare arms. She opened her eyes sleepily, her gaze meeting the gentle tawny stare of the lion, his head resting against her thighs, his body stretched languidly on the grass. He gently rubbed his head against her stomach and her fingers stroked the soft mane. Daniel knew. He would protect her.

She slipped into a doze, her fingers entwined in his fur.

When she awoke he had gone and she thought for a moment she had been dreaming but then, as she scrambled to her feet, she noticed the golden hairs clinging to her jeans and, smiling, she brushed them onto the indented grass.

Suddenly the pain hit her and she bent double, gasping.

"Tom…" Her cry tailed into a wail as another contraction hit her.

It was time.

* * * * * * * * * *

Freya looked down at the new-born babe in her arms, wrapped in a soft, white shawl. His tiny fingers escaped the mesh of wool and she gazed into the round, un-focused eyes. His tuft of fair hair tickled her cheek as she bent to kiss him. A deep wave of love enveloped her.

The midwife stepped aside as Tom crept to her bedside and, bending over, caressed the cheek of his son. "He's beautiful," he whispered. "So beautiful." His fingers gently explored the button nose and tiny lips. "We'll name him after Ethan. Don't you think?" He smiled at Freya.

"Ethan?" she whispered.

He nodded, his gaze returning to the baby. "A family name – and it was Ethan who brought us together."

"Ethan." Freya gazed at the child in her arms and felt the pain of protective love.

Outside Leofric Farm, the wind whispered through the baby branches of the apple tree and then circled slowly to the clouds, which split, releasing sun beams that caressed Daniel, the celestial power animal, slumbering on the grass, guarding his new young soul-mate.

Also by Fay Wentworth

Collections of short stories

Destiny's Footprints

Twist & Mix

Romantic Mystery

Sweet Destiny

Chase a Rainbow

Winds of Change

Runaway Love

Suspense

Tangled Web

Paranormal

Shadow of a Memory

Are you Lost?

www.faywentworth.wordpress.com

70873321R00058

Made in the USA
Columbia, SC
15 May 2017